EVERY SEVEN YEARS
and
I DON'T REMEMBER

Two Books

CINDY I. WILSON

 FriesenPress

One Printers Way
Altona, MB R0G 0B0
Canada

www.friesenpress.com

Disclaimer: The story "Every Seven Years" is a total work of fiction. Any specific facts stated about the Vietnam war are my memories, not necessarily accurate facts.

ISBN
978-1-03-832530-3 (Hardcover)
978-1-03-832529-7 (Paperback)
978-1-03-832531-0 (eBook)

1. FICTION, SHORT STORIES (SINGLE AUTHOR)

Distributed to the trade by The Ingram Book Company

BOOK ONE

Every Seven Years

BOOK ONE

EVERY SEVEN YEARS

Table of Contents

Chapter One:
First Love

My grandmother always said that every seven years things change. It could be your health or the circumstances of your life. But, change would be inevitable. Sometimes for better, sometimes for worse.

I was seventeen years old in 1967. If you lived on the Canadian prairies in the 1960's as I did, you were about as far removed from the Vietnam War with the United States as it was possible to be. Most teenagers in the small towns and cities of the Canadian prairies had no connection to the war in Vietnam. They knew a war was going on, but then as now, most teenagers had little interest in the news on radio or TV. Almost certainly, they never read the newspapers. Most Canadian teenagers, were too busy participating in the peaceful sixties ideals of "flower power" and "free love" to worry about a war thousands of miles away. "Flower power" basically meaning not worrying about making things happen. It was believed good thoughts and the tides of the universe would steer the world in the right direction. Also the sixties was the time of the "free love" philosophy. "Free love" meaning sharing love (sex) with anyone who "struck your fancy" through a haze of pot smoke. (The fear and knowledge of AIDS was in the future).

These sixties ideals were exemplified by the now famous Woodstock concert and the hippie communes set up in rural areas throughout the United States as well as some in Canada. In the communes everyone lived together on one plot of land, not hindered or harassed by government interference. In these communes the hippies happily raised families with children having names such as Moon Beam, Harmony, Echo, Karma, Rain, and Leaf just to list a few. Often the parentage of each child was unknown due to the "free love" aspect of commune life. Therefore, many commune children considered multiple commune members to possibly be their parents.

On the Canadian prairies, dotted with smaller cities and small towns, we generally didn't have communes, and pot was not as readily available to youth on the Canadian prairies as it was in some of the larger U. S. states. We didn't have "ban the bra" marches where bare-breasted women marched to receive equality with men in the workplace. We also weren't involved as the U. S. was, in the marches to de-segregate black and white schools and de-segregate black and white in all aspects of society. The black population in Canada was fairly small when compared to the United States. And definitely very small on the Canadian prairies.

On the Canadian prairies most youthful and cultural rebellion of the sixties amounted to some subversive pot smoking in basements and at parties, guys wearing "love beads", lots of beer drinking, and an overly large percentage of teenagers wearing tie-dyed t-shirts with a large PEACE sign on the front. The sixties was supposedly the era of love and peace. And actually, on the Canadian prairies that was pretty much true. The sixties of pot-smoking, communes, and marches was almost over before its effects were finally felt on the Canadian prairies in the early seventies.

Of course, even as teenagers, we did have knowledge of the war in Vietnam. But our friends and brothers weren't dying. So, although we felt some kinship and empathy for those young men who died in the dense and terrifying jungles of Vietnam, as well as for their families, we were set apart at great distance from their tragedies. In 1967, the war in Vietnam was still a continuing horror, suffered by the people of the United States. In Canada it was merely a backdrop for the culture changing sixties.

The sixties was a great time to be young in Canada. The country was prospering. The prairies were thriving, youth was driving society, and in music the Beatles singing group was making us all "feel fine.

Draft dodgers and the war in Vietnam were definitely not top of mind for most Canadian teenagers on the prairies of Saskatchewan in the sixties. Our closest link to the Vietnam war was through what appeared to be an inordinately large number of young men of American backgrounds who became professors and session lecturers at our universities. Of course, we students didn't know for sure that these instructors were draft dodgers; vital young men who'd burned their draft cards to escape service in Vietnam. But, when we discussed it among ourselves in the university student lounge, the definite consensus was that these young professors and instructors were in Canada because they had dodged the draft. With no verified facts but with the surety of youth we knew we were right.

At the time young American men were dodging the draft my grandparents rented a house they owned to a young couple. The young couple said they were married and were from British Columbia, Canada. They were very vague on the details of their life. But, in the sixties people were often more trusting, some would even say naïve. My grandparents thought they "seemed like a nice young couple" and so without seeing any credentials they rented the house to the young couple. As time went on my grandparents noticed the couple never had visitors or friends stopping by, never received any mail delivered, and didn't appear to have jobs. My grandparents came to the conclusion the young man was probably a draft dodger. The wife was probably not his wife, but his girlfriend. The couple seemed to be about eighteen or nineteen and too young to be independently wealthy. It was likely that someone was sending them money to allow them to live without jobs. The mystery of the very quiet, almost invisible couple, was solved when an Amnesty program was offered for a short time frame, by the United States government. It allowed draft dodgers to return home with no legal repercussions. And voila! A few days later, during the night, the couple disappeared! A rent cheque was left in my grandparents' mail box. My grandparents were pretty sure they had been harbouring their very own draft dodger. And as they did not agree with the war in Vietnam that was just fine with them.

The Vietnam war divided U. S. families and communities. Some citizens believed it was a righteous war, one that must be fought. Those families believed their sons must sign up with the military and join the fight. They believed their young men had to do their duty and become part of the war in Vietnam.

On the "other side of the coin" some families believed it was a war that should not be fought and could not be won. And their young men should not have to participate. As the war dragged on so many young American men were killed that eventually there was a draft lottery. All young men between the ages of 18 and 26 were in the draft lottery and could be drafted to fight in Vietnam. This was a lottery you did not want to win.

There were some special circumstances that disqualified you from going to Vietnam, such as physical or mental disabilities, or if you were going to college. If you were going to college you could put off being in the draft lottery until you were 26. When you turned 26 you could be conscripted to go to Vietnam. These young men had no choice.— Well, in reality there was one other choice. The choice was they could dodge the draft by fleeing the United States. When making that choice, some young men had the blessing of their families. Other young men who made the choice to flee the draft were totally disowned by their families. Those families thought it was a cowardly and unpatriotic act on the part of the young man to flee. Those families thought that all young men should do their duty and fight for the United states in Vietnam.

A large number of those who dodged the draft crossed the border into Canada (approximately 30,000), where in Canadian towns and cities they quietly waited out the Vietnam War. After the war many draft dodgers did not return home to the United states. Those that stayed in Canada benefited Canadian society by becoming politicians, environmental activists, and teachers.

By the summer of 1967 the war in Vietnam was still being endured by the people of the United States. In contrast, my summer at the lake in 1967 was wonderful. That summer I met a boy; a man really. He was nineteen, with clear hazel eyes framed by eyelashes any girl would envy, and sandy hair that fell to one side above a strong angular face. He was so handsome he took my breath away. His name was Mitchell Travers and I liked his smile from the first minute I saw him. He was older than I was, so I was flattered, almost stunned, when he seemed to take a liking to me. That summer at the lake, Mitchell Travers and I became inseparable.

It wasn't surprising I was at the lake that summer. From the time I was three years old, from April to October my family spent every weekend, and my dad's work holidays at the lake. When it was cold weather my dad had the fireplace blazing both during the day and all night in the large main room. When the weather was hot every window was open. And as the cottage was on the top of a hill cool air blew in off the water a mile away.

The old cottage my parents bought was on Last Mountain Lake, fondly called Long Lake by the locals. It was long-seventy miles long. My dad was a prairie boy who had joined the Navy in the Second World War. Going from wheat fields to the ocean he had developed a love of being near the water. So, my parents scrimped and saved to buy an old summer cottage within very short walking distance of the lake.

The summer I met Mitchell Travers was magic. Our summer together must have been destined by fate. Because from the time I turned fifteen, I worked as a clerk in a small local drugstore store. I worked in the store part-time during the school year and throughout the summer, with weekends off. I wouldn't normally be able to spend the whole summer holiday at the lake. But this particular summer my boss had some serious health issues and was closing down the drugstore and taking the entire summer off. Bad luck for him, good luck for me!

This very special summer when Mitch and I met, Mitch was working for rotund Eddie Metz at the small grocery store/restaurant near the beach. He was living in what was originally the small summer kitchen out back. Mitch was a great cook. Much better than Eddie ever was. Mitch cooked thick juicy burgers, which could be eaten inside in the two windowed booths along the front of the store, or could be carried to the screened-in verandah along the main front entrance of the building. Because of Mitch I'd bet more hamburgers were sold that summer than ever before. The tiny restaurant was hoppin'. Chubby Eddie, who usually ran the place alone in the summer months, was considering retiring and so decided to hire some help. Which couldn't have worked out better for me! That fact brought Mitch to the lake. Eddie had certainly never drawn the volume of female patrons that Mitch was bringing into the restaurant. And of course, where the girls were, the boys were also. Eddie was having a very successful summer that year!

No one knew too much about Mitch. His speech had a slight western drawl and he had the rangy good looks of a cowboy. He never gave a direct reply to questions about his home or family. He just diverted the questions with a joke or noncommittal answer. We were all so enthralled with him for his easygoing charm and totally irreverent wit, that we never pushed for specifics. He was older; a man of the world who was emulated by the boys, and sought out by the girls. For some reason he was drawn to me. Of all the cool girls and goofy kids who gravitated to the store that summer, Mitch took to me.

We were an unlikely pair in many ways. I was probably considered by some of our group to be too quiet and not stunningly good-looking enough to attract Mitch. I did have nice brown eyes in what was considered to be a heart-shaped face. My chin length hair was blonde-brown and I wasn't very tall. But Mitch seemed to think I was perfect. And that was definitely good enough for me. From the first day we met, there was a spark. Not only was there a total sexual attraction, that gently and constantly pulled us close, but the same things struck us as funny. The first day I met Mitch he was flipping burgers on the grill. And he made me laugh with the first words he said when he asked me if I wanted my burger to "moo", or be like a blackened piece of charcoal. I was in love from that moment on. Mitchell Travers and Katie Kristoff were in love.

I took to dropping by the store during the day to see Mitch. I couldn't get enough of him. I'd leave my friends lazing on their towels on the beach. I'd slip into the restaurant to edge up close to him at the end of the serving counter, where I could hold his hand beneath the tiled counter overhang. Every evening I walked down from our cottage to meet him at 9 o'clock when the restaurant closed. In the sixties in our beach community, many people were still outside late into the evening. The narrow main road was well lit and well populated on both sides. So, perhaps again naively, in the sixties, it was assumed to be safe for a young girl to be walking to a destination by herself at dusk. And as Mitch walked me home later my parents felt they didn't have to worry.

When I reached the store and opened the rickety, creaking screen door Mitch was waiting for me. He'd lock up. Then Mitch would take my hand and wrap the strong fingers of his comfortable grip around it. We'd walk a few yards from the store to sit shoulder- to- shoulder on a grassy bluff, which in front of us, fell away to a rocky point. The point protruded into the water about thirty feet below us. To the right of our lofty perch we could see the last of the sun seekers now sitting around a bonfire on the shore or standing in small groups, talking and laughing. To the left of us, by the light of the moon and a canopy of stars, miles of a crystal blue lake sparkled like a thin sheet of silver that shimmered ever so slightly with even the softest breeze.

Families had headed back to their cottages hours ago. But the teenagers wanted to hang out together as long as possible. From their time at the lake these young people had built friendships and lasting relationships that would continue into adulthood. As Mitch and I sat in the encroaching darkness and the evening closed in around us, we took the opportunity to hug, kiss, and murmur softly about the happenings of the day. Then, before we got too close, and things got too serious Mitch would walk me back to our cottage. The walk included more hugging, kissing and shared soft laughter, with one last lingering kiss at my back door, followed by promises of tomorrow.

Summer seemed to be endless. It was filled with a constant stream of sunny days. On the water the sailboats with their bowed sails, the fishermen with their small outboards, and the die hard water skiers were always trying to squeeze the last ounce of enjoyment out of a great day on the water. On the beach the sun worshippers, drowsy with eyes closed, were lulled by the soft sounds of the rise and fall of the tide against the sandy shore. Or, as they lay close on their towels, they were speaking to each other quietly as they confided some tid-bit of interesting information, or gave an update on some previous conversation. That conversation of course, might contain some snippets of juicy gossip. The dedicated sun-worshippers often stayed until the sun started to dip below the horizon.

As for Mitch and I, we were living totally in the present. We were so wrapped up in each other we didn't look past the serene days of summer. When we were together our talk was of beach activities, the beach crowd with their crazy antics, and deciding what to do that evening. We were enclosed in the warm cocoon of new love. Although we seldom spoke of the future, when we did we just assumed we would be together. I still had a year of high school to make a decision on what I wanted to do. Mitch said his plans were uncertain. He would decide what to do at the end of the summer – which seemed to be a pretty vague plan. Especially for someone like Mitch who could be very definite and could be very focused. I decided I wasn't going to worry about his vague answer. In my heart I knew whatever plans Mitch made, they would include me. So I put thoughts of the future out of my mind and lived fully in the moment of summer.

Behind the bluff where we always sat, slightly to the west of the store, was a large two-story building we called the Hall. It had been built in the twenties, concurrent with the building of the store, and had always been a meeting place for the beach community. Over the years, Saturday night dances, socials, weddings, anniversaries, and birthdays, had all taken place in the Hall. Now only the main floor was used. The old wooden floor of the second storey was considered unsafe. Now the Hall was mainly used by teenagers on warm summer evenings. The live bands of yesterday had been replaced by a jukebox and the large dance floor was now partially covered by ping-pong tables. It didn't matter that the Hall lacked the glory of days gone by and smelled slightly of dried lumber and dust. It was still the place to be when evening settled in, and the blue velvet night called seductively to youthful pleasure seekers.

Everyone between twelve and twenty met at the Hall. They either stayed there for the evening, or left from there for other entertainments. In the sixties, many of those other entertainments revolved around beer. The bonfires in the "grove" deep in the trees to the east of the Hall, generally involved beer and beer craziness, as did the late night swims, and the car rides to party destinations. We felt the unquestionable invincibility of the young. The intelligent ideas of

MADD and SADD and designated drivers had not yet been formalized and promoted.

Mitch and I were part of it all. He had a crazy sense of humour and eyes that smouldered sexuality when he directed them at you, and only you. When I was with Mitch, everything was exciting; everything was summer romance perfect. I'd never spent a better summer. Mitch met my family and surprisingly they liked him. My parents thought he was a little old for me, but as he seemed like such a decent guy and fitted in so well with my brothers and their friends, he was just accepted as " one of the kids".

I did learn that Mitch's parents lived in Wyoming and he had an older brother and a younger sister. It was the evening after I'd introduced him to my family that I learned more about his. We were sitting close together on the bench outside the Hall when Mitch abruptly started to speak. He said he had been very close to his older brother and was still very close to his younger sister. When I asked why he was no longer close to his brother his face lost all expression. He looked straight ahead. His eyes focused on something that wasn't there. He told me his brother was dead. Then he added, after a short pause, that his brother's name was Jesse. I asked what had happened. Mitch answered in a quiet, controlled voice, that there had been a terrible accident and he really didn't want to talk about it. We left it at that, he holding his secret close and me not wanting to intrude on his privacy. After a moment he continued, softly stating that his brother had died two months ago. When Mitch finished his terse discourse with that added information, there was complete silence between us. I didn't know what to say. I was young. I had never been confronted by the death of someone close to me. I was at a loss to know what to say to comfort him. So, I just reached for Mitch's hand and said nothing. I didn't want to make him feel worse. He looked to be in such misery that it seemed he couldn't find the words to say anything further. We just sat shoulder to shoulder wrapped in silence. The "hey you guys" call from another couple by the Hall broke the quiet stillness and Mitch snapped out of the trance he'd been in to smile at me and then wave at them.

The evening progressed as usual. We put the sadness away. When we joined the group by the Hall, there was plenty of "goofy kid stuff", and lots of just plain silliness. Lots of laughing and some practical jokes that were of the good clean fun variety. There was always a couple of livewire jokesters that were telling slightly off-colour jokes or playing pranks. Maybe someone's cap disappeared and finally, after much finger pointing it finally reappeared in the sweatshirt hood of some unsuspecting innocent bystander. In general the beach crowd was a pretty nice group. Maybe some were wealthier than others, with better cars or just had any car period. It was mostly a middle income group that hung out at the Hall. The few kids with lots of money often took off back to the city for their evening fun. The group wanting more rowdy or intimate fun gathered in the wooded "grove" where activities involved a lot of beer, pot smoking, and entry level sexual activity. Mitch and I were in the group that stayed near, or in the Hall.

We were living in the moment which was being embraced by kids high on life, enjoying a carefree summer in the sun. The realization that there had been a tragedy in Mitch's life added a deeper dimension to the respect I felt for him. He certainly wasn't a whiner. His quick wit and quirky sense of humour hid a depth of feeling he didn't openly display. The golden days of summer continued. For me nothing could have improved on them. And Mitchell Travers was the reason.

I was seventeen and I was in love; truly, deeply and forever in love. Mitch and I didn't speak of it. We didn't analyze it. We just felt it. I knew in my heart it was the same for Mitch. I knew it was endless and could only get stronger.

Our idyll of young love came to an abrupt end that summer in the last week of August-August 31st to be exact. It was a Saturday night and our group along with some others, had congregated at the Hall. Teenagers had spilled out onto the gravel parking area, the adjacent grass, the top of the bluff, and the steps of the store. Mellow, yellow, light from the tall old windows in the Hall, as well as a golden August moon, softly illuminated our secure little world. The music of the jukebox in the background helped to give a party atmosphere to the summer night.

Chapter Two:
Things Changed

The RCMP cruiser which softly crunched onto the gravel in front of the store and turned off its lights, was barely noticed until two uniformed officers came leisurely striding up to the door of the Hall. As if on cue, the song on the jukebox finished and the attention of all those outside became directed at the officers. In 1967 at our beach, only the most dire of circumstances would warrant the police making a trip out from the city. I don't think I'd seen a police car at the beach more than three, perhaps four times in my beach lifetime.

Mitch and I had been sitting on the grass beside the Hall doing a little kissing, a little hugging, and a little silly whispering like sweethearts do, when the police pulled up. As the music on the jukebox stopped and a crowd gathered, I stood up to see what was going on. I leaned around against the corner of the building so that I could hear what the officers were saying. I reached my hand back to pull Mitch with me. Mitchell Travers wasn't there. I thought he was just kidding around, disappearing in the shadows behind the Hall so I'd come looking for him. Then I thought maybe he'd gone back to his old red Chevy to get a jacket or a coke. But with the first question the stockier of the two officers asked, I got a bad feeling in the pit of my stomach. He wanted to know if there was a Brett Fairmore in the group. Someone had reported seeing him with a group of kids near the Hall last night. The other officer held up a coloured photo of Brett Fairmore. It was Mitch. The print underneath the picture said Brett was a draft dodger who was wanted by the U. S. military for his part in a terrorist attack in Wyoming. He was to be considered extremely dangerous. Do not approach him. Call your local RCMP detachment immediately. After the first stunned moments caused by recognition of the face in the picture, several kids spoke at once identifying the face as that of Mitch Travers. Inevitably the questions drew me into the spotlight. When I had given as much information as I could, I was given a lift home in the police cruiser and my family was also questioned with an admonition to call if Mitch contacted us. The police seemed satisfied with our answers and went merrily on their way after unwittingly shattering my little world. No wonder Mitch's plans were undecided. He was a draft dodger and a wanted terrorist on the run. It was bad enough to be suffering total disbelief that the U. S. military and the RCMP were looking for Mitch, but my stunned disappointment, coupled with the terrible sense of loss I felt, was overwhelming. I felt betrayed, used, lost, and utterly desolate. Deep within my soul I had felt inextricably joined to Mitchell Travers. I just believed there was a tie that would always connect us. The bond I felt for Mitchell Travers would always remain even if his name was Brett Fairmore.

For three days the local paper carried articles about a young draft dodger terrorist from Wyoming and the unsuccessful efforts of the U. S. military, local, and national police forces, to locate and capture him. The articles were repetitive and gave very limited details about the terrorist crime Brett Fairmore had been involved in. The police investigation seemed to be at a standstill. Each article was accompanied by a head and shoulders photograph, probably from a high school year book, showing a clear- eyed, good- looking young man with a great smile. I could barely make myself read the articles, yet I couldn't resist the pull of news, good or bad about Mitch. (To me he would never be Brett.) The police never did give specific details of the terrorist attack Mitch was supposedly involved in. The fact that Mitch was considered dangerous was alarming and also absolutely impossible to believe. After a few days the news cycle moved on to something new. Mitch was barely mentioned in the back section of the paper. His story lost importance, then quietly disappeared.

As my grandmother said, there are major changes that take place in our lives every seven years. I became a believer in that "old wives" tale because it certainly seemed to be true in my case. I had grown up and made a good life for myself in the seven years since Mitch had disappeared. Then something very unusual happened. Seven years after Mitchell Travers dropped out of sight, on August 31st, I received a delivery of lovely yellow roses and a short handwritten note. The script was a firm scrawl with an angular slope and clearly formed letters which were occasionally graced by an artistic flaring finish. Just the kind of script I had often seen on food orders at a small beach store seven years before. The note was unsigned and simply stated that I had been on the writer's mind many, many, times and hopefully I was doing well. I knew it was from Mitch. The handwriting was Mitch, as was the simple, concise message.

In the seven years since Mitch had disappeared, the news from the United states told us that the Vietnam war was finally drawing to a close. Amnesty had been offered to all the young men who had become draft dodgers and had fled their country rather than participate in a war they could not in good conscience support. Activists who had resorted to violence, trying to stem the tide of young men's blood from America flowing away to nothing, through the jungles and rice paddies of Vietnam, were held accountable, and then forgotten. The world was changing.

Until I received the card that day, and read the short note that came with the roses I thought I had put the summer of Mitch out of my mind. The short, heartfelt note broke my heart. Until I received it, I hadn't realized I'd been holding myself close, still waiting for something, or more correctly someone, as impossible and as unrealistic as that seemed.

Chapter Three:
Grandmother's Sayings

I don't know why Mitch sent me a message after seven years. The length of time could have been a coincidence. We often did laugh at some of my grandmother's sayings. And one of her favourites was that life changes every seven years. She had one for almost every occurrence. Like "throwing salt over your left shoulder to keep unhappiness from entering your house". Or that "finding a penny would bring good luck". Or that "breaking a mirror would bring seven years bad luck. However, if you put the pieces back together your luck would be restored". Or that if you could "skip" a flat stone across the water you would be lucky in some way. My grandmother always said these old sayings with " tongue in cheek" and with a twinkle in her eye. But the one saying that she actually did believe, was that every seven years life changes. She always said that she had seen it happen time and time again. And Mitch was familiar with that saying because one night we had debated whether that could possibly be true. When he sent the flowers perhaps things were about to change for him and he hoped that I might be included in those changes. The roses were a lovely surprise, but really what was the point? They couldn't replace actually seeing Mitch. And at that particular moment, no change including Mitch did develop. It was a mystery with no answer.

My life continued on. It was good; ordinary, but good. I had friends and a secure job at an accounting firm. In winter I enjoyed taking my nieces and nephew skiing. Although we lived in a flat prairie province the retreat of the glaciers in prehistoric times had carved out a very long, very beautiful valley with steep hillsides that was only thirty-five minutes from the city. One area of that beautiful valley had been developed into a local ski hill. The skiing was great with a small chairlift and variable runs suitable for various levels of ability. My nieces and nephew excelled at the sport at an amazing rate. When summer came I could be found enjoying cottage life in the family cottage near the water. I remained close to my family and saw them often. I had taken sailing lessons at the local sailing club and I had bought a little skiff. It was a lot of fun to sail it up and down along the shore line. And there was always someone who wanted to go for a ride. It often crossed my mind that this was the same lake where Mitch and I had found each other.

I had always been a "doodler" drawing small pictures in the margins of school reports or on notices, or letters written to friends. In the seven years after Mitch left I translated my doodling into actual pieces of art. I painted people and florals. But my real love I discovered, was abstract art. I loved choosing the perfect mix of colours. I loved getting the symmetry of the lines just right and the weight of the printed objects used as accents, equal on both sides of the painting, to give the correct visual appeal.

I enjoyed my job in accounting but my art gave me chances to travel nationally and internationally. It was great to have the success and recognition. However, I would have to say I also enjoyed the money I received from every sale! And no matter how many paintings I sold I always got a real thrill out of the knowledge that someone liked my art enough, that they were willing to actually pay for it!

The only thing I really seemed to be lacking was that one great true love. Over the years there had been some good sweethearts, even some very good sweethearts but no one who could be considered a truly great love. I guess in my heart I was hoping that somehow I'd find someone who could strike a chord within me as Mitch had. I still longed to see him although the logical part of my brain told me Mitch and I had no hope of ever meeting again.

In the seven years since Mitch left I had stumbled into a profession I totally enjoyed. I had always been a math person. So accounting was a perfect match for me. The numbers told the truth. If manipulated and used properly the outcome with numbers was always satisfactory. Which is not what could be said about real life experiences. I was pretty content with life in general.

Chapter Four:
My Brother's Friend

Unbelievably, two weeks after I received the roses and the anonymous note my life did change. I ran into Danny Collins, my older brother James' best friend. He was one of a small number of young Canadians who had joined American soldiers to fight in Vietnam. When I was a kid, long before I met Mitch, I had always had a huge crush on Danny. Of course, he never bothered with me as I was just James' kid sister. Consequently I could only worship Danny from afar. Danny and I had always had something in common. We were both "math brains". Something which eventually found us both working with numbers. My brother James, who was so smart in many areas, could not relate to math. James was a very smart guy, but with math of any type he was at a loss. Numbers were not his friend.

Danny Collins, James Kristoff, and Jay and Brendan Taylor had always been best buddies, in good times or bad, from kindergarten to grade twelve. Although I was two years younger, and a girl, my brother James and I were close. James often let me tag-along with him and his buddies when their adventures were just clean fun, nothing with an edge to them that would bring us close to getting into any kind of trouble. After high school James went to college and studied languages to become an international interpreter. Jay became a highly qualified electrician in charge of managing large projects throughout the province. Brendan became well known, and in much demand, for his ability to completely rebuild or repair very high end vehicles. Danny took a very different path.

Growing up with a severe lack of money in his household, Danny had lacked opportunities other kids took for granted. In comparison to our household full of love and respect Danny's home life was the complete opposite. Which is why my parents always included Danny, as much as possible, into our family. When Danny's father did happen to notice, which wasn't often, he wasn't happy about Danny being at our house all the time. So my parents did as much as they could for Danny without making his life at home with his father worse. I know my dad often slipped Danny some spending money, as well as money for some groceries, or something he needed, like a new pair of shoes.

As to why Danny signed up? He never did say. I think some of it was youthful idealism about trying to save the world. Also the enticement of leaving a small city for the first time and seeing some of the big wide world. Something he would never have hopes of doing on his own. Then meeting with a smooth talking, charismatic U. S. recruiter who emphasized all the pros of signing up such as; respect given to those in military service, and that same respect opening pathways to good career options. And also extremely appealing to an underprivileged kid like Danny, was the opportunity to have a regular paycheque of good wages coming in. Money that could be saved to build a nest egg to procure a start to a secure financial future. Add to that the slick U. S. recruitment campaign which painted a picture of having a proud military career, and the nobility of helping to save the world from the encroaching evil of communism by defeating communist North Vietnam-and Danny was sold.

It didn't take long after Danny arrived in Vietnam to discover that all that talk of future respect and money earned in the military dwindled severely in comparison to the fact of just trying to survive daily in the jungle. Four young men who were best friends; three building a future at home. One veering off onto a very different path far away.

It was a shock to see Danny. Oh, he was still a big strong- looking guy and very handsome. With his dark hair, and blazing blue eyes, set in a ruggedly handsome face, he had always had the wow factor. Unfortunately, he had not come back from Vietnam unscathed. He came home with serious injuries. Some were visible to the eye, like his slight limp caused by a back injury, and the small mortar shell burns he had suffered on the lower side of his face and neck. Some injuries were not visible. I learned later the terrors Danny saw and participated in while in Vietnam haunted him, often causing spells of depression, anxiety, and terrible, continuing nightmares.

When Danny saw me he picked me up in a big bear hug lifting me off the ground.

He said, "What the heck Katie Kristoff? You're still as light as a feather". Guess you never did get that growth spurt you were always hoping for!"

Relative to Danny's 6'1" height my 5'2" was pretty negligible.

I laughed and said, " You know the saying, 'good things come in small packages."

As he smiled at me his smile still had that same "knock your socks off " effect as it always had. We decided to catch up over coffee. And after coffee we decided to get together again a week later. Danny was still the wonderful guy I remembered. He still had that charisma. It was like some invisible force pulling you toward him into the golden circle of his smile. He was one very attractive guy. I was so glad that Danny and I had met. My girlhood dreams come true. I felt badly that he had been injured and was having a hard time. Danny said when he first came home he hadn't been able to work because of his injuries. He had been living in a hostel. But his leg was gradually getting stronger and he had been promised a job doing the books in the office of a local business. The job even had the possibility of an eventual promotion. That was quite a big deal. Many Canadian business owners who thought the war in Vietnam was a waste of time, money, and human life, had no interest in helping returning Canadian Vietnam vets. These business owners generally had a poor opinion of anyone, who had volunteered to fight in Vietnam. In their mind the thought was, "Why would anyone volunteer for a war that could not be won and had no effect on Canadians and Canada's immediate future?" Very often the respect returning Canadian Vietnam vets were hoping for because of their military service, was not only missing. It was also often replaced by either pity, or even in some cases ridicule. These Canadian Vietnam vets got no respect for possibly throwing their lives away for some other country's very poorly thought out unwinnable war. Therefore, as in the U. S. some returning Canadian Vietnam vets fell upon hard times and became homeless. Drug addiction from their time in the horrors of the Vietnam war also contributed to homelessness for returning Vietnam vets in Canada, as it did in the U. S. Danny was basically homeless because of his minimal income. He was living in a hostel until he started the job he felt very fortunate to get. Thankfully, drug addiction was not a problem Danny returned home with.

When I left Danny with our plans in place to meet later in the week, I got to thinking that although I did enjoy my position at the accounting firm, perhaps a job at the Veterans hospital would be more rewarding. Maybe with my financial skills there was a chance to help some of the young men, who like Danny, were just so young when they made a decision that placed them in an unthinkably awful situation. And if they did return from Vietnam, their lives were often never what they had hoped their lives would be. Finding a job or accessing funds could be difficult. Perhaps with my financial and accounting skills I could help Canadian Vietnam veterans access financial aid and set them up so that the finances they did have, could work to the best advantage for them.

The next week I made an appointment to meet with the director of the Veterans Hospital. The director felt my skills would be better suited to working with the Veterans Association rather than the hospital. He immediately set up an interview for me with the director of the Veterans Association. The interview went very well and I was offered a position.

My decision was quickly made. I quit my job at the accounting firm and after two weeks off I reported to my new, tiny, windowless office in the Veterans Association financial wing.

I liked the job. Though it was often tinged with sadness for the mental and physical disabilities of many of the clients, it was also satisfying to know I was helping very deserving men and women find their way to financial security.

Things were going well with Danny and I. I was "head over heels" in love and Danny seemed to be having the same feelings. Between us there was a strong physical attraction like a single flame drawing you closer and closer to the bonfire. The foundation for our love story was a history of friendship, respect, and also a similarity of background. So many things were in our favour to turn our finding each other into something great. Our world was starting to revolve around one another.

Danny and I enjoyed many of the same things. I still saw my brother James' friends, Jay and Brendan and their wives and children on a regular basis. Danny became a part of that. We also both thought my brother James was the "best" and we saw him often.

Danny and I liked to swim, so we were at the community pool at least once a week. And unbelievably I'd found a man who liked to dance! How great was that! His grandmother had taught him when he was a kid telling him being able to dance was the way to a lady's heart. We enjoyed going to movies at the movie theatre, not so much watching them at home. We went to plays-nothing sad, mostly comedies or musicals. We walked all year long, bundled up to our ears in the cold or "skinnied" down to shorts and T-shirts in the heat. We liked to read the weekend newspapers together with endless cups of coffee on Saturday mornings. We rode our bikes on all the trails around the city and in the huge city parks.

We both preferred to live in an older area of the city. That's where the condo we bought together was located. It was within walking distance of bars and small cafes. It was an area where we could also take the Light Rail Transit to our jobs. And best of all about being with Danny, besides sharing such a strong love, was that we had fun together. Though Danny was such a sophisticated, upper echelon, executive- looking, kind of guy, his personality didn't match his looks. He liked to laugh. Danny had a great sense of humour. He had lightening speed hilarious wit. He could always see a different twist or take on something to make it seem amusing. We laughed a lot.

We were living very close to a perfect life. When we talked of the future we always included plans for raising a family one day. Of course Danny couldn't always be joking and jovial after surviving the terrors of Vietnam. There were times Danny did drift into silence, his mind travelling back to the horrific jungles of Vietnam. The times Danny did get silent and distant I would sit right up close to his side, take his hand, and share his silence. These tortured silences happened less and less as everyday life took precedence over the past. Danny slowly and gradually seemed to be managing his recovery from his wartime experiences. Or possibly, he was just hiding his past so well I believed what I was seeing. Once I did gently mention it might be beneficial for him to get counselling. He was not interested. So, I decided to take his acceptance of the past at face value. He knew I was by his side if he ever needed support.

Life was going so well. Then one evening he didn't come home from work. When I finally called him he wasn't answering his phone, so I left a message. I didn't get a reply. That was a bit worrying because although he now mostly appeared to be a sunny kind of guy

Danny still did suffer from some underlying depression as lingering results of his time in Vietnam. I was getting worried. Sadly, Danny had no family in his life I could call. His father had passed away while Danny was in Vietnam. And his mother had immediately left for parts unknown, leaving no forwarding address. I called several of his buddies but no one had seen him.

Horribly, the next day, Danny was found lying in a damp and weedy, empty field on the outskirts of the city. He had been shot execution style with one fatal shot to his forehead. How could that be? My shock was overwhelming. That was impossible to believe. Danny was a likeable, hard-working, clean-living guy. Who could possibly want to do something so senselessly brutal to my loving Danny. The police had no clue what had happened. Over the coming weeks their investigation went nowhere.

I was so stunned I was walking around in a fog. I was devastated. I had started to believe Danny and I would be having a great life together, forever. I had always really, really liked Danny when I was a kid. And now I had grown to really, really love Danny. Even as a kid Danny had been magic to me. He was so totally appealing with his charm, his laughter, his quiet confidence, and his good-hearted nature. As time passed and there seemed to be no answers to Danny's death I trudged through my job and my sadness to find consolation in my work.

Eventually after months of sadness the pain of loss started to fade slightly. I began going out with my girlfriends again, joining in some group activities, and going to the odd get- together. But truthfully, Danny was never far from my mind. The way he had died was so terrible it was hard to eliminate or even diminish the memory of it.

Chapter Five:
Life Moves On

One year after Danny's death I had a job offer of a new position in another city less than five hours away from where Danny and I had shared a home. I would be running an outreach program using my financial expertise to help returning Canadian Vietnam vets work with U. S. government programs to get their deserved benefits and also to re-set their finances. I would also be helping these Canadians get any kind of assistance available from the Canadian government to help them move on with their lives. The job was a little unusual as I was a mediator and go- between working with both the U. S. and Canadian governments. It was often very easy for the U. S. military and the U. S. government to forget the Canadians who had contributed to the war effort in Vietnam. It was a fine dance to find ways to proceed. The job would be a challenge but also I thought, very interesting. Because this new position would be in a city nearby it would have dual positives. I would still be able to see my family regularly as well as start a new adventure. I could possibly make some new friends- maybe even find love again. It would be nice to have a change. Most of my close friends were married with children and very involved in family life and their children's activities. I was on the outside looking in. It was time for me to find some new experiences and hopefully build some new relationships.

I took the job. I settled into a condo, once again choosing a quiet, older area of this city that was new to me. The condo was close enough to allow me to walk to work. One of the nice perks of this job was that the very small department I worked in was part of a much larger department, which had a very active roster set up for group activities and special occasion activities. Many people joined in or attended the diversely different activities offered. It was part of a work place initiative to help build camaraderie and common interests through the job.

I wasn't really a "joiner" but I was drawn into a running group and a "movie night out" group. I always thought I'd like to be a "runner" instead of a "walker" so I took a chance and I liked it. The movie group was fun and involved supper before or after the movie with a little beer or wine included. Over time I made some solid friendships and went out on some nice, but not special dates. I had the best of both worlds, still close to my family, but enjoying something new. I was comfortably adjusting to my new life.

One of the vets I worked with was Peter Jensen. It came to light, that during his time in Vietnam he and Danny had been best buddies and had been in the same unit. It was nice to have contact with a friend of Danny's. But for me it also dredged up the sadness I had tried to bury because Danny was gone. I think it made Pete feel comfortable talking to me as he knew I had been important to Danny. Apparently he and Danny had kept in touch since they had returned home. That was news to me. Danny had never mentioned Pete.

Some months after Pete became my client the unthinkable happened. Pete had been found on the outskirts of the city. He had been killed with one shot to the forehead execution style. What was going on? That was exactly like Danny's death. And they had been friends and they had both served in the same unit in Vietnam. That seemed to be quite a coincidence. Best buddies in the same unit in Vietnam who were both killed execution style when they returned to Canada. I couldn't wrap my head around it. It was an odd connection and was more than a little disturbing. It was just impossible to grasp. It was just so awful.

Because I had been working with Pete I was interviewed very thoroughly by the police. There was a sad pall over our department because many of my colleagues knew Pete. He was an extremely personable, friendly, guy. – always sharing a comment or joke with a staff member as they walked by while he was sitting waiting for his appointment. Though he may have been broken on the inside he hid it well. And although suffering mentally from the results of his Vietnam experience he was trying to move forward with the help of counselling. It was a heart-breaking ending to a life that had suffered through adversity and was trying very hard to beat it.

When the police were looking through their files to find any previous cases with identical circumstances my name showed up as having been interviewed about both Danny and Pete's deaths. So the police came back to talk to me.

The police officers were very tight- lipped about why they were asking for information on Peter Jensen and Danny Collins. They kept asking if Danny had mentioned anything about illegal trading in black market products in the last camp where he and Pete had been stationed. There had been rumours of violent deaths in the two villages near the camp. The officers said the way Danny and Pete had been murdered was indicative of an organized crime hit. Perhaps while stationed in that particular camp they had seen something or had heard something they shouldn't have. The police officers did say that as a rule the Canadian police wouldn't have been looking into something that might have happened in Viet Nam. That would be stepping on the toes of the U. S. Military. But a lead from an unknown source had said Danny and Pete might have known some-thing relating to an upcoming military trial in the U. S. The U. S.

military, in this case, had asked for assistance from the Canadian police to follow up on that lead.

I told the police officers I didn't know that Danny and Pete were in contact after they returned to Canada. Danny had never discussed Pete with me. I had never heard Danny mention Pete. I only met Pete after Danny was gone. As I had no information of any value to share with them the officers said their goodbyes and left.

When the officers took their leave I was left with the distinct impression that something must have happened that obviously wasn't good, and that Danny had been involved in it in Vietnam. And it seemed whatever Danny may have been involved in was probably something criminal in nature. That was impossible to believe. Danny had an open, honest nature. Criminality just wasn't part of his character. I did realize however, in horrific times of war sometimes the norms of an ordinary life were hard to maintain.

There really wasn't anything I could have added to the police investigation. I hadn't noticed anything out of the ordinary. I hadn't even known that Danny and Pete were best friends and had kept in touch. I only learned that information when Pete became my client. Which made me doubt slightly, how well I had really known Danny. I didn't like that thought so I put it aside.

I was doing my best to move on from Danny's death and the identical death of Pete. So, when my birthday came along I was very pleased when a group I worked with took me out to a ritzy restaurant for dinner and drinks to celebrate. Because two of the guys with us were Vietnam vets the question by one of the younger associates about the war brought up some interesting conversations. The two vets enlightened us with a few stories of the black market trade during the Vietnam War and how very dangerous it could be. Participating in black market trading would be considered treason by the U. S. military because that trade of American goods like gasoline or ammunition, even food rations, could help sustain the enemy, and therefore help to kill American troops. Vietnamese criminal associations brokered the deals. These deals could be very lucrative to individuals in the American military if they were willing to take the risk for big cash rewards. Odd that Danny had never mentioned anything about U.S. troops being involved in black market activities. Although I guess it really wasn't odd. Because Danny didn't talk about anything to do with Vietnam. When we first got together and I asked about something I'd seen on the news about the war. He said, for him Vietnam and everything associated with it was in the past. He would never want to talk about his war experiences. He said that was the only way he could deal with his service in Vietnam. I knew the path he was taking was not the path to good mental health. However, everyone is different. Danny seemed to be able to compartmentalize and close off that part of his life in order to enjoy life in the present. He still had nightmares, and short periods of depression, but he seemed to have found a way to survive the past and look to the future, our future. I did worry that he should be seeing a professional so that someday he wouldn't become overwhelmed by the past. But we were so in love and everything was so good, I wasn't going to rock the boat by suggesting what path he should take to get over the trauma of war. In the end it didn't matter. Danny was gone and my life had to go on.

Life continued to move along

Chapter Six:
A New Love

I became a doting aunt to my three nieces and one nephew. As we now didn't live in the same city I didn't see them as often as I would have liked too.

I kept up with them mostly through letters and gifts, some very expensive long distance phone calls on special occasions, and "every so often" in- person visits. I was beginning to see time marching on with me having no one special in my life. Then on August 31st fourteen years after Mitch disappeared I received a beautiful bouquet of yellow roses. What the heck! The roses were accompanied by the same short handwritten note. The script was a firm scrawl with an angular slope and clearly formed letters which were occasionally graced by an artistic flowing finish. The note was unsigned and simply stated that I had been on the writer's mind many, many, times and hopefully I was doing well. I knew who the note was from. Unbelievable! Seven years to the day again I received yellow roses! Suddenly in my mind I could see a great smile, clear hazel eyes, and hear a voice with a slight western drawl. For just a moment my mind drifted back to warm summer nights, warm arms around me, and the euphoria of complete happiness. Why had Mitch been accused of such terrible things? It was still an open question with apparently no answer. And also, why didn't he contact me in any way except with yellow roses every seven years. And would my grandmother's saying come true again? Would life change?

Yes. Her saying did come true once again. Things did change. I met a man.

I was at my usual coffee shop. I often stopped there after picking up a few groceries. I liked to have a cup of Americana coffee in my favourite window seat, where I could watch the hustle and bustle of the world going by. On this bright afternoon filled with sunshine, when trees and flowers were in full bloom, I met a man. I don't know why I first noticed him. He was not overly tall. He had light brown hair and eyes a perfectly ordinary shade of brown behind round tortoise shell glasses. He wasn't a man who would particularly stand out in a crowd. But he seemed quietly self-assured and friendly as he gave his order at the counter. He seemed to have the quiet confidence of a man who was comfortable in his own skin. His voice had a warm huskiness. And there was something about him that just screamed "nice".

I turned my attention once more to my coffee. Then suddenly as this man with the light brown hair and round tortoiseshell glasses was passing my table his foot caught on the edge of my chair, which in turn caused an amazing juggling act between a covered cup of coffee and a large sticky bun. When the juggling act stopped the coffee and sticky bun were sitting on the edge of my table. When I caught the eye of the juggler we both started laughing. The juggler had a great laugh and a great smile. His very ordinary brown eyes sparkled with laughter. In the pause after the excitement the juggler said, "Hi I'm Robert, but my friends call me Rob. Is this seat taken"?

With a continuing smile I said, "Nope. It's all yours. It's not every day I'm entertained by a classic juggling act."

"Well," Rob continued, " It does take practise."

As he sat across from me he said, "It seems as if I should know you as I've seen you here so often ."

" Yes. I do stop here regularly. I like to sit in this window and watch the people passing by. There's always something interesting to look at." I replied.

"My condo is just down the block. So this place is pretty handy for me. And the coffee and snacks are always good," Rob added.

" I like to shop in the area," I said. "And for sure, this coffee shop is a gem. Because I like to shop locally, I regularly walk to the "Italian Market" for my groceries. It's a little longer walk than to some of the shops around here, but I like the walk and I like the products."

"I go there quite often." I continued. "Then I usually stop in here for coffee. So I'm pretty much a regular."

"I guess I'm a bit on the lazy side," said Rob. "I like to shop at the "Shop Way" that's almost right beside us. It's got everything I need and it's so close that it makes getting groceries a lot less painful. I like to cook but I'm not a fan of grocery shopping".

"I'm the opposite," I replied. "I don't mind buying groceries, but I'm not much of a cook. Which is why I don't have too much for groceries, to weigh me down on the return trip home from the market. I've fallen into the bad habit of going out for a quick meal two or three times a week. I'm a regular at "Mama Joan's Home Cooking". Although it's quite a distance from my condo, the prices are good, and the staff is lovely, as is Mama Joan. The food really is like home cooking. I often vow I'll cook more. But I never seem to follow through with the idea".

"I'll have to try Mama Joan's sometime. It sounds like a place I'd enjoy. A restaurant that serves meals that taste like home cooking is a real treasure. I do like to cook," added Rob. "But it's always nice to have a good meal out."

"As far as grocery shopping goes, it's a good thing I live close by," Rob continued with a smile. "I always end up with too much when I go to the grocery store. By the time I get home my arm is about three inches longer my bag is so heavy. "

I laughed and said, "I know exactly what you mean. Although I don't buy a lot, I always end up with more than I planned to buy."

Rob continued, " I teach psychology at the university so I'm here a lot. Do you live close by?"

"Yes." I replied. "And I work in the Veterans Services building just around the corner. I've been working there for a while now and I really like the job. This coffee shop is very handy. Perhaps too handy sometimes. Those sticky buns are hard to resist and I'm often taking one home with me. It's a good thing I joined a running club at work. It means I can eat one of those sticky buns and still try to run it off."

" I'm a runner too," said Rob. " I started several years ago. I run every evening after work. As you live close by and we both like to run maybe we could go together some evening. "

"That sounds like a nice idea," I smiled. "Sometimes it's so much nicer to run with someone else. Also, there's safety in numbers. Every so often when I cross paths with someone who looks a bit sketchy I feel a shiver of apprehension. I'm sure they are fine. And I've never been bothered. But they just don't look like someone I'd want for a pal," I laughed.

"By the way. My name is Katie", I said.

"Pleased to meet you Katie," said Rob. "Do you think you would want to meet to go running this weekend? I can meet you at the coffee shop around 11:00 and we could go in the morning instead of you going by yourself later. I usually do run after work, but on the week-ends I always go about 11:00".

"Yes, thanks. I would like that. I have to get going. I'll leave you to your bun and coffee and I'll see you here on Saturday at 11:00. It was nice meeting you Rob." I smiled.

"And it was very nice meeting you Katie. I look forward to Saturday. See you then," said Rob as he returned my smile.

My footsteps were so light they were filled with air as I walked the few blocks to my condo. Things were looking up. Maybe something good was going to happen. Maybe that seven year change idea of my grandmother's was true. Perhaps there was romance in my future.

Life changed after I met Rob. First we became running buddies, going running three times a week after work. Then after a few weeks we added a Saturday date, usually lunch and a movie. As often as possible, we packed a picnic lunch and spent the afternoon in one of the large parks within walking distance in the area. We were becoming close. Then one Saturday evening after dinner we went back to Rob's place and sealed our relationship with more than hugging and kissing. We found passion. We were great together. Our lovemaking that evening was a pledge for a new beginning. Maybe there wasn't the fire for me there had been with me and Danny but this new togetherness with Rob was lovely. He was a kind, humorous, loving man. And I was so lucky to have found him. Eventually it came out that he was a draft dodger who had decided to stay in Canada. In his case his parents were supportive and were all for him dodging the draft.

The Christmas after we met we travelled to New York to spend Christmas with his mom and dad, two sisters, and her kids. It was a very nice Christmas. In the next few years we often went and spent time with his family. I grew to love them all. They were so warm and welcoming. They were a special enhancement to my life. As a person coming from a smaller city in Canada, amazingly, I grew to love the city of New York. It provided seemingly never-ending delights with shopping, the arts, the ocean, so many possibilities. I knew Rob missed the familiarity of New York and his family, but he seemed happy with the life he had made in Canada. Like many draft dodgers who built lives and stayed in Canada he seemed pretty content with his choice.

As time went on we built a happy, satisfying life. I still did some painting and sold paintings but I wasn't as involved as I had been.

We had chosen Rob's condo to settle in as it was situated better than mine was for both our jobs. Rob and I took some great vacations to warmer climates in the winter. We particularly enjoyed Mexico, staying in the same hotel every time we visited. We both enjoyed winter so we skied in the Canadian Rocky Mountains staying in chalets in Banff or Lake Louise. We both grew up spending time at a lake or in Rob's case near the ocean. Rob's parents had a much more luxurious "cottage" than my parents had and it was oceanfront property. Plus, they had all the toys: a speed boat for water skiing, four jet skis, assorted kayaks, and a small sailboat. We spent the evenings enjoying barbecues on the deck. And then as night closed in there was a huge fire in their fire pit on the ocean shoreline. A stay at the Winston's "cottage" was a magical event filled with family and extended family with a sprinkle of long time friends thrown in. Everyone was very welcoming to me. They were lovely people but sometimes I did feel a little out of my depth. After all, I was from a middle income family with middle income values. I'd grown up within a much different lifestyle than Rob had.

Rob and I decided to look for a small place on a local lake. As it would be only the two of us using it, it didn't need to be large. One sunny afternoon we saw a for sale sign on a front lawn. The cottage on the lot was looking old and worn but the view and the lake front location was fantastic. We both thought the place was full of possibilities. We figured re-doing the cottage would be a good project for us. It took a lot of weekends and some help from friends but the result of our hard work was a comfortable, cozy, hideaway. We were proud of, and thrilled with, the end result of our endeavour. It was also winterized. What a plus for the cold, snowy, Saskatchewan prairie winters. I'm sure the Winstons (their name even sounded wealthy) probably thought our little cottage was not up to snuff. They likely thought it was not of high enough quality for their son. But Rob's parents were fine, kind, people. They were very gracious on the one and only time they visited Canada, to visit our smaller

Canadian city, and our humble lake cottage. For them nothing could compare to the United States. They were American through and through. And I definitely knew, no small city in Canada could in any way compare to the wonders they knew in the city of New York. I didn't let it bother me much – that feeling of not being quite good enough. Because I had Rob and they didn't.

Rob and I had decided rather than putting all our money into a house in the city we would keep the condo and enjoy our lake retreat instead. We spent a lot of happy hours doing "do it yourself" projects on the cottage and being by the water. We eventually bought a little rowboat, in honour of one I had as a kid. It wasn't anything Rob was used to, as most of his water toys had motors. But he really did seem to enjoy our little rowboat. We painted it bright purple and had such fun following along the shoreline for miles with it. And because our travel was so quiet we could get up close to all kinds of birds and animals that lived near or along the shore; mink, weasels, deer, bluebirds, geese and ducks. Any animals from foxes, to bobcats, to moose, that drank from the lake water could be seen from our little boat. And with the rowboat we could go from the cottage to the main swimming beach in about ten minutes which was much quicker than travelling the roundabout, winding gravel road to get there. We could leave the rowboat pulled up on the shore by some trees and shrubs below the cottage when we were done with it, which was very convenient. No need for a boathouse. We could loop the rope around a tree and leave it. It was a small beach community without much theft so we weren't concerned about one day finding it missing.

Our jobs were good, our trips were good. Our life at the lake was great. Our lives were stable and satisfying and we still had fun together. Which was such an amazing aspect of our life. Our enjoyment in each other hadn't dwindled over time. In my mind we had the best life! And after a slow start to full blown romance it turned out I was crazy in love with the guy!

Occasionally we spoke of marriage but then asked ourselves. "Why?" We were very happy as we were and we had been together long enough that in the eyes of the law we were married. The only thing we never spoke much about was children. Rob wasn't ready at the time we first discussed it and I was very happy as we were. As time went on I began to think a little boy or girl of our own would be nice. And my biological clock was starting to tick a little. But Rob always gently put off the discussion of children. At first he said he wanted us to be more financially secure. We were pretty financially secure. Then he said his job would be changing and would involve a great deal more stress. He had already had several changes in his job which he had taken in stride, showing no signs of stress. Also, he felt with children we would have to cut back on our travelling which he felt we would miss. I wouldn't miss it enough to forget about children.

Eventually the topic of children was put on the back burner. I tried to put thoughts of children away and just be glad I had a great partner like Rob and a very good life. But I couldn't quite do it. And although the topic of children was seldom mentioned it started to put a tiny wedge in our relationship. Rob was great with his sister's kids. So, it was hard to understand why a loving person like Rob would not love to have a child. I couldn't figure it out. His explanations seemed unrealistic.

About a year after our last real discussion of children took place Rob went on a business trip to New York. When he came home he was quiet and distant. A couple of months later he went on another business trip to New York. Then he hit me with it. He was leaving and going back home, as he called it, to New York. I thought he was home. I thought being with me was home. I thought home was with me in Canada.

It turned out that on that first trip to New York Rob had run into a girlfriend from his previous life in a local coffee shop. It seems coffee shops can change the direction of lives. Who would have guessed! This girlfriend had been his first true love in high school. They had drifted apart when they both won scholarships to colleges at opposite ends of the country. When this girlfriend from a previous life completed her degree she was offered a teaching position as a professor in the Psychology department of the same college she had attended. Then two years ago she had moved back to New York.

When Rob finished college he moved to Canada to dodge the draft. And even after amnesty was given to draft dodgers by the U. S. government he decided to stay in Canada rather than return to the U. S.. On his first business trip to New York he and this previous girlfriend had gotten together for coffee and lunches. Then on his second fictitious business trip to New York, they had apparently spent every moment they could together. And voila! Love bloomed with such intensity that Rob was ready to throw everything we had away! Throw me and our life away! In one week he was gone. He resigned his position at the university. His clothes, his bike, his home office disappeared "pfft", as if by magic. Disappeared so quickly it seemed as if he was gone in the "blink of an eye". My life was in ruins in the "blink of an eye". He did tell me how sorry he was. How he felt terrible at betraying our love. He said just one look at this woman from his past and he realized what his life had been missing. I didn't realize our life had been missing anything. I was frozen in place. After he left I had to force myself to go back to the condo every day after work. I couldn't stand to be there without him. I wanted to sell the place and get out. I just couldn't do it. I kept waiting, thinking he would come back. He would realize what a mistake he'd made, what a hole he'd left in my life.

It never happened. Rob never came back. His old girlfriend was obviously from a society family as Rob was. And I guess the pull of that society upbringing made an old bond of romance when renewed, even stronger. After some months I sold the condo and moved. A few months after Rob left my lawyers had been contacted by Rob. It was decided we would split the sale price of the condo and that I should retain ownership of the lake cottage. I really didn't know how I would ever go back to the lake.

That year Christmas was very different than previous years. There was no visit to New York. No dazzling New York displays of decorative lights outlining the shops and downtown streets. No skating with a handsome man under a star filled sky, at the ice rink in Rockefeller Center, within the coloured glow of the majestic well-lit huge centre piece evergreen tree. There was no Christmas shopping in exclusive New York shops while being lulled by soft traditional Christmas music. And there were no extravagantly wrapped Christmas packages filling the arms of me and a handsome man after Christmas shopping in the hustle and bustle of New York City. There was no sharing the anticipation of Christmas with someone special. I guess in my years spent with Rob I'd grown accustomed to all that Christmas in New York provided. I'd grown accustomed to the glitz and glam of the "Winston New York Christmas". To make my misery complete a blizzard attacked the city and I could not make the trip to be with my family. I had no one to share the day with. Talk about a bleak, grey day. Christmas passed.

The next months we're horrible. Unhappiness struck me at every turn. Rob was a kind, loving guy. I knew his love for me had been real. I guess just not real enough to win out over someone from the past. I finally told myself to buck up and get on with my life. This kind of heartbreak happened to people every day. I told myself I should use my own expertise and the coping strategies I taught my clients to help me get over this drastic change in my life. Many of my clients' situations were so much worse than mine. And many were finally coping with the new reality of their life. That resolve helped put my pain in perspective.

Chapter Seven:
Danny and Pete's Story

Life moved on. I still had a job I found satisfying. I still had my family close by, my running group and my movie group. And I was advancing at work. With that advancement came the opportunity to become the key note speaker at conferences around the country. Surprisingly that was something I enjoyed. I wasn't really an extrovert but I did believe in my subject and I did hope my practises and insights would be useful to those at the conferences.

I had just had another birthday and occasionally felt a bit like success in my personal life might be passing me by. I often thought it would be nice to meet someone special at one of these conferences. As it turned out I did meet someone special but it was a new friend named Sally Mason, not a new sweetheart. Sally was a Canadian Vietnam vet. She had been in the same unit as Danny and Pete. She knew them well. Wow! Talk about a coincidence. As the three of them were Canadians from the prairies, in a sea of Americans, they had formed an immediate bond. This bond only grew stronger as their tour of duty continued. Sally and I spent a lot of time together over the three day conference and continued our friendship when we returned home. Over time we became very close. We became best of friends, as close as sisters. And as I had no sisters, she was a lovely addition to my life

Sally was on her own too. As with me her family lived in a different part of the province. Sally rounded out my life. It was great to have her to spend time with. She was a cheerful, optimistic person. Which in itself is such a gift in a friend. She was also an adventurous person, as you'd expect, taking into account she voluntarily joined the American military to go to Vietnam. I couldn't really understand why she'd do such a thing until I learned that Sally's family was American. She had been born in Canada and therefore had Canadian citizenship. But a large part of her family and all her relatives were in the States. And they were all on the side of the U. S. government and very pro Vietnam war. Two of Sally's cousins signed up and Sally(very foolishly she realized too late) signed up with them. They believed all the U. S. promotion and propaganda about the war with Vietnam. They thought they were going to do something important with the United States to help stop the spread of communism.

With Sally I found new things I liked to do, such as camping beside rivers I'd never seen, and kayaking for miles along uninhabited shorelines. Things I had never done. I became adventurous also. We took our holidays together and travelled on our own to smaller out of the way places in Mexico, Portugal and Spain, to find some of the hidden charms of these countries. In Mexico we went ziplining across tall jungle canopies of foliage. Pretty much any idea Sally came up with, I was game to try. All her ideas made life more interesting. Whether it was trying to roller skate at a new roller rink or singing karaoke at a small local bar. Knowing Sally showed me I was more adventurous than I thought I was.

Although, looking back I did do a few risky things following my brother James and Danny's lead when I was a kid. James and Danny would let me go along with them for activities they thought were safe. The operative word here being "thought". We put pennies on the railroad tracks to see them flattened, then kept them like trophies.

James and Danny got the swinging bridge over a big creek near our house, swinging as high as possible, and then the three of us like three unsteady drunks, stumbled across it. When James and Danny jumped into the lake from the highest promontory point above the lake I followed. When they climbed the highest tree in the back-yard to spy on the neighbours I followed. And when they let me sit between them on James toboggan careening down the steepest hill in the valley I was thrilled to be squashed in between them. And also thrilled we were lucky enough to survive the crash at the bottom. Things I never would have done on my own, I did because I was with James and Danny. I would have followed them anywhere. I guess Sally tapped into that adventurous side I'd always had, but which had lain dormant until she came along.

I felt very lucky to have found Sally for a friend. Of course Sally knew about Mitch, and the roses and the seven year changes. Being a common sense kind of person she thought you should live in the present, not look back into the past. She had been married, then divorced. Obviously she hadn't fallen for anyone at a young age, as hard as I had fallen for Mitch. Though I didn't often think about it, I still had feelings for Mitch tucked away safely in my heart and mind, in case he should ever return.

One evening as Sally and I were sitting on my balcony, each with a glass of wine, we were discussing how Danny and Pete had died and going over again, the still hard to believe details of their deaths. Sally had liked them both very much. And like me, she still couldn't believe they were dead; and that they had died in such a shocking manner. After we had become so close, Sally had told me how at the end of their tour of duty, Danny and Pete had been playing with fire. Luckily they had gotten out of Vietnam without getting burned.

Sally had told me that in the last month of their tour Danny and Pete had gotten involved in a deal to transport black market goods to the Vietcong. These were supplies the Vietcong was in desperate need of. Danny and Pete had been approached by one of the men in their unit about making some black market runs. This man was secretly the broker between the black market operative and the military unit.

Danny and Pete had heard horror stories from incoming American recruits about how things were getting so much worse for American vets returning home, the longer the war in Vietnam went on. Those American vets returning who were not disabled and could work, often couldn't get jobs. Many employers who were against the war wouldn't hire anyone who had been a part of it. Homelessness for returning vets was becoming a very real problem in the U. S. In Canada the threat of these problems was much more minimal. Yet there were also some horror stories of returning Canadian Vietnam vets having problems getting jobs or financial assistance. Plus, in some cases there was a lot of negativity, and lack of respect, for Canadians who had gone to fight in an American war that basically wasn't considered to be a Canadian problem. Danny had no family to help him out if he came upon hard times after he returned home to Canada. Pete had a family, but they had been totally against him signing up to fight in a war that was an American problem. His parents had never been supportive of him in any way before he made the decision to sign up, so it wasn't surprising they didn't support Pete in this. He knew that if he came home and needed a helping hand from his family, none would be offered. Being in similar situations Danny and Pete feared there was a possibility they could be looking at a bleak, empty, future when they returned home to Canada. If like many American vets, they couldn't get jobs, they would have very little income and the spectre of becoming homeless was a real, and terrifying, worry hanging over their heads. So, for big money, they agreed to make a one time delivery of supplies other than weapons, ammunition, or gasoline to the black market operative. They would only deliver items like medicine or food. These were items that would not directly kill American troops. Although realistically, keeping the Vietcong fed and healthy would be indirectly killing American troops.

The Vietcong operative must have been desperate for supplies because he agreed to their terms. In their hearts Danny and Pete knew that delivering these non-life threatening items instead of ammunition or gasoline didn't excuse making a deal with the enemy. But the very real fear of being a young person facing a harsh and hopeless future can make you do things you normally wouldn't even consider doing. They both had no family to give them support. And Danny and Pete were definitely afraid of what their future might be when they returned home.

As the delivery date for the black market goods neared Danny and Pete started to rethink their deal. For only one delivery they could be set up with enough money for a start on a good life when they returned home. However, at the last minute their patriotism and care for their comrades, made them change their mind. The deliveries they had agreed to make, although not life threatening, would still help to sustain the lives of the enemy. They decided to back out of the deal. By a stroke of luck and a twist of fate the group of Vietcong fighters Danny and Pete would have had to deal with, and who would not have been happy about them changing their minds, seemingly disappeared, moving out of the area to fight elsewhere. So Danny and Pete were free and clear with no reprisals from them. And the soldier on the base who had brokered their deal was killed out on patrol, so there would also be no repercussions from him for them deciding to withdraw from the deal. Danny and Pete didn't wish death on anyone of course, but maybe this soldier's bad deeds against American soldiers had brought Karma back on him. His death certainly helped Danny and Pete get out of a very bad agreement free and clear. The downside of backing out of the Vietcong deal, was that now their plan to earn big money to provide a good base for their futures was gone. They would have to hope for some good luck and some opportunities to present themselves when they got home.

A few days after getting free of their black market deal, on one of their reconnaissance patrols looking for Vietcong fighters, Danny and Pete patrolled near two villages. These two villages were close to the base. They didn't see any fighters, but they did see villages that had been decimated by warfare. The villagers were barely sustaining themselves. The children in particular were suffering. They were looking frail and malnourished. This war, as in any war, was ruining the lives of ordinary citizens. As Danny and Pete were turning the Jeep to drive back to camp an old man ran out in front of the Jeep. He spoke very little, very broken English, but with the help of hand signals and a few English words he was begging for help for his village. He was asking for food staples like flour, powdered milk and rice, as well as some basic tools for rebuilding the two destroyed villages. As the old man was talking he uncurled his hand and showed Danny and Pete a handful of small rocks. Pete recognized what they were immediately. The summer before Pete signed up to go to Vietnam he and two buddies had gone on a trip to British Columbia in Canada, where they spent a week in the mountains trying their hand at panning for gold. It was a trip run through a travel agency. And they actually did find a couple of gold nuggets. They had a great time. Who would have thought that being able to recognize which piece of ordinary looking rock was a gold nugget would be a valuable skill to have? Danny and Pete made a deal with the old man. They would deliver the goods the next day and the old man would pay them in gold nuggets.

When Danny and Pete returned to the base, although not saying anything about the gold nuggets they had seen, they asked the Vietnamese interpreter at the base about the abandoned mine near the two villages. The interpreter gave them quite a history lesson. He said all the men in those two villages had worked in the gold mine. He did know that although the mine had been closed down long before the war started, those who had worked in the mine knew where to find any small veins of gold that had been left behind after the final clean up. It was a huge mine and the very small veins of gold were considered unimportant to the large mining operation. The company was after the large veins only, which were more economically and less time consumingly feasible, to concentrate on. And when the large veins dried up the mine was shut down. The company went bankrupt and disappeared.

The interpreter continued with his information saying, their familiarity with the mine allowed the men from the villages insight into where to find the many small, and very small veins of gold that remained. It was a huge mine. The men from the villages had found enough small veins of gold over the years to develop a lucrative business. The interpreter said that before the war these particular villagers, from these two villages, had been well known throughout Vietnam and Southeast Asia. They were known as craftsmen and artisans who changed raw gold into highly desired gold jewelry.

Though they were on the outskirts of the jungle the two villages were not ordinary villages. These villages were very large and well- populated. These villagers were productive, wealthy, and well-respected. The two villages through their trade in gold jewellery, helped provide economic stability for the area. These two villages were much more than unwanted obstacles in the U.S. military's march to winning the war. Although, realistically, it would have made no difference whether the U.S. military did or did not know what it was destroying. These two villages were just a bump on the supposed road to victory by the American army. Even if the army's top brass had realized that the villagers were talented artisans who were providing a sustainable life to a large population of innocent civilians, it would have made no difference. These villages and villagers, like so many others, became collateral damage in the path of the United States march to defeat the Vietcong.

Danny and Pete actually thought they were doing something for humanitarian good helping the villagers. The supplies they were taking to the villagers would have very little impact on the U. S. war effort, but would have a great impact on the villages. And those gold nuggets offered by the old man could secure their future. Danny and Pete also felt that taking these supplies to the villagers would be a sort of penance of doing something good in the war. As opposed to their first plan to secure their future financial security; by participating in the black market providing food and medicine to the Vietcong. Those supplies of food and medicine would have helped keep Vietcong fighters alive, which in turn would have killed American and Canadian soldiers. How could they have ever thought they could do something like that? It was such an ill-thought out plan. They were not those kind of people. Danny and Pete wouldn't have been able to live with that decision. And thankfully, they realized the enormity of that bad decision just in time to get out of the deal.

Danny and Pete took Sally into their confidence after she saw them heading out on an extra unscheduled patrol. They asked her if she wanted in on the deal but she declined. She told them it was too risky. Even though they were doing something good, the exchange of military goods for gold could get them all court martialled. But, she would keep their secret.

Sally saw Danny and Pete return later that day. She saw them very hurriedly park the jeep behind the unit supply building and stealthily and rapidly unload the supplies they had taken for the villagers. Apparently they hadn't delivered them. As she watched Danny and Pete took off at lightning speed into their barracks. They looked very stressed and upset. Sally figured something must have gone wrong with their delivery.

Sally continued her story for Katie; Things had gone terribly wrong. Danny and Pete had made their first run to deliver the goods to the villagers. They had planned the delivery for two weeks before they were to be deployed back home to the States. As they were nearing the first village they heard shouting and gunfire, which was unusual to say the least. Then to see two senior officers from their unit being the cause of the disturbance was a surreal sight. Their unit was stationed where there was little interaction with the Vietcong. But still, the last thing you wanted to do was alert any stray Vietcong fighters who may have slipped back into the area. Obviously the officers making the noise were so furious they were displaying unwise recklessness and a very poor lack of judgement. They were tempting disaster with all that noise. Danny and Pete pulled back into the deep foliage to keep out of sight. They then crept closer to hear what was being said. They saw the two senior officers from their unit shouting, and then shooting several shots very close to the head of the man they were beating. It was the old man from the village that Danny and Pete had made the gold deal with. Danny and Pete moved close enough to hear what the officers were saying. The officers wanted to know if the old man had any gold. They had been told two villages in this specific area were involved in producing products made of high grade gold and they wanted some of that gold. Finally the old man agreed to get them some and crawled into his home with the officers following him, kicking him viciously as he moved. Five minutes later there was gunfire, a woman's screams, and the cries of children coming from inside the home. Then more gunfire. Then absolute silence. Almost immediately the two officers walked out of the home patting each other on the back, smiling, and each carrying a small leather pouch.

Danny and Pete waited until the officers were gone to be sure they wouldn't be seen. Then they hurriedly made their way over to the old man's hut. What a horrific scene. A whole family dead. There was nothing they could do for the family. They definitely couldn't risk staying around and getting caught in a fire fight with the enemy. Almost certainly the Vietcong would also have heard the shots and come to do reconnaissance of the area. They had to get out of there.

Sure enough, while they were heading back to their Jeep the jungle came alive with Vietcong fighters. It was a miracle they made it to the Jeep without being seen. They started it up and drove like the devil himself was chasing them through the Vietnamese jungle undergrowth and made it back to the base. When Sally went to talk to them upon their return they told her what had happened. As two high ranking officers were involved, and Danny, Sally, and Pete were all on the bottom of the military totem pole, it would be their word against the word of the top military brass if they told their story. Who would believe them? And they only had two weeks to survive the war until they went home. There was no way they wanted to endanger that timeline. So why rock the boat? There was no way anything they reported would work in their favour. They were due to go home and leave the army behind. They didn't want to do anything to change that outcome. The three of them made a pact that the events of that day in Vietnam would never be spoken of again.

When Sally left that evening I felt very unsettled. Could the way Danny and Pete had been killed have anything to do with their ill-fated attempts to engage in illegal activities in Vietnam, first with the black market and then with the old man from the village. Though really, as they hadn't actually made any deliveries to the villages that seemed a pretty far-fetched connection. No one other than Sally knew anything about what they had been trying to do. Their time in the war was over. They were home safe in Canada. Their time and experiences in Vietnam were behind them and that's where they wanted them to stay. They should have been safe in Canada.

It kind of bothered me that Danny had gotten involved in something illegal. It didn't seem like him. But then again I had never been fighting in a jungle war, in a foreign country, in brutal, and mind-altering combat. So who was I to judge. And I didn't have night-marish fears as Danny and Pete did, about what awaited me when I returned home. I just knew Danny was a loving, sweet, and kind person who had filled my life with so much joy, and so much love for a short period of time. And that was how I would remember him.

For days I couldn't get what Sally had told me out of my mind. I finally accepted that as there was nothing I could do about the mystery of Danny and Pete's deaths, I would have to leave it in the hands of the police. Hopefully some day they would be able to solve the case. It remained an open case. Eventually I found I could remove myself from thoughts of the past and move on.

That seemed to work until one day after work Sally called me with some news. The mystery of the execution style deaths of Danny and Pete was finally solved. Danny and Pete thought no one had seen them leave the gruesome crime scene at the villager's hut. They were wrong. The two officers who committed the crime had seen the Jeep's tail lights and with a little research had discovered who was driving that Jeep. However, as Danny and Pete kept quiet (who would believe them?)and Danny and Pete never accused them, the officers decided to bury their crimes with silence.

Everything changed when those two officers were charged with war crimes. They couldn't take the chance that Danny and Pete would testify against them. So they had them murdered.

Unfortunately for the two officers, killing Danny and Pete didn't stop the march of justice. Other witnesses to their crimes came forward. Two men from the village where the deaths had occurred had gone to the Vietnamese and U. S governments saying they were willing to testify against the officers. When Sally heard the two senior officers were going to trial she volunteered to come forward to tell what she knew. She was taking a risk after the fate suffered by Danny and Pete for knowing too much, but she would remain anonymous until she appeared as a surprise witness for the prosecution. The last to testify. As no one would know beforehand of her testimony the risk of any backlash to her would be minimized. And her risk did pay off. With Sally's testimony giving Danny and Pete's recounting of the events of that bloody day, along with testimony from the two men from the village, the fate of the two officers was sealed. The two officers were convicted. They would never see the outside of prison walls.

Danny and Pete had done something illegal they never would have done at home. Sadly Danny and Pete who were such special young men, were just two of the many casualties, in one way or another, of the futile war in the violent jungles of Vietnam.

Hearing this news from Sally, that justice had been done, gave me some peace and brought back memories of laughter and great love for Danny. I had loved that man for so many reasons, starting from the time we were children. I often saw his face with a loving smile, when a lovely memory of him and me would slip across my mind. His death was such a violent end to a life of promise and the end of a beautiful chapter in my life. Of course I also felt renewed sadness at Pete's death but it didn't come with the same hurt and pain. I only knew Pete as a very nice person, as my client. Sad as it was to think of Danny and Pete's deaths the mystery being solved did bring some closure.

Chapter Eight:
Earth Shattering News

Time moved on and when August came again I was once more at the lake visiting with my family. I was once again, as in times gone by, sitting on the grassy bluff overlooking the lake. This time I had one arm around the solid little body of my youngest niece and the other arm around the solid, shaggy little body of Freddie her black and white mutt. The bluff and the rocky point were the same but the Hall was gone, as was the store. A dusty parking lot now occupied those spots. As my niece, and I, and Freddie, sat in companionable silence, a carload of kids in a beat up old blue Ford convertible parked on the gravelled parking lot behind us acting like happy- go- lucky idiots. Some running joke they were enjoying with hilarity went on and on as the local station blasted pop tunes which the group enjoyed at the highest volume possible. Over the hilarity of teenage laughter I heard the work whistle, which the radio station played as a signal that it was noon, and that the national news was about to begin. The kids were laughing and carrying on so much I don't think they realized or even cared that the music had stopped and the news had begun.

The volume was so loud on the car radio I could clearly hear the introduction to the news program. The first news item rocked my world. The announcer stated that one of the longest running unsolved crimes related to the Vietnam War had finally come to a satisfactory conclusion. The investigation had been active since 1967. Today, a fourth person involved in the 1967 bombing of a Wyoming firm making munitions for the Vietnam War had come forward and cleared Brett Fairmore. Brett was the younger brother of the protester Jesse Fairmore, who had been killed in that bombing attack. The last activist and fourth co-conspirator in the bombing, had come forward when he was promised he would receive a minimal sentence if he provided information that would help solve the case. This fourth co-conspirator was now having psychological problems which stemmed back to his tour of duty in Vietnam before he had participated in the bombing. He was also carrying a heavy load of guilt because he had let the reputation and life of young man named Brett Fairmore be destroyed by his silence. And all these years later his stress had become totally overwhelming. This final activist, the fourth man, finally felt he had to set the record straight to clear an innocent young man as well as clear his mind.

The pop tunes returned. The laughter increased and the engine revved. Dust and gravel spit like hail in a huge beige arc as the carload of teens took off. In the ensuing silence I just sat perfectly still, letting my niece babble on and her dog doze. My body was statue still but my mind was playing and replaying every word the announcer had said. Many emotions spilled into my mind. There were feelings of hope and exultation; then a deep sadness for what might have been in my life, and for the ruination of a wonderful young man's life.

That night I returned home and bought every newspaper I could get my hands on. Sure enough, in every paper there was a photo of Brett Fairmore who looked very solemn with his charming smile missing, but with the same clear gaze focused on the person who was speaking. In each newspaper it was the same photo. Brett's hand was being shaken by the governor of his home state of Wyoming. In each newspaper the article under the picture, along with the apology being offered to Brett for being wrongly accused with no real evidence, also told of a compensation package. The package was great, but how do you replace the youthful joy and hopeful prospects taken from a young man at nineteen years of age.

I found one in- depth article that explained the facts surrounding the bombing of the munitions factory in Wyoming, and told why Brett Fairmore had been labelled a terrorist.

Brett Fairmore had merely been a kid who thought the world of his older brother. On that fateful evening in 1967 he had dropped his brother and three friends off at an old two storey house four blocks away from the Fenwood Munitions Factory. He'd given them a ride in his red Chevy. He thought they were meeting some girls to go camping. That's why they had the duffel bags and heavy jackets. He was just a gullible kid who thought his brother Jesse and his friends were going on a secretive overnight camp-out with a bunch of hot women.

After the bombing, and Jesse's death, one of Jesse's friends and his co-conspirator had implicated Brett through a deal cooked up as part of a plea bargain that would work to that friend's benefit at trial. One co-conspirator had evaded police capture and remained at large. And although Jesse's other friend and third co-conspirator had constantly and consistently denied Brett was involved, the prosecutor decided to try to diffuse some of the public's outrage over the terrorist attack on home soil by taking Brett into custody. In panic, Brett fled, thereby appearing to be guilty. To make matters worse, Jesse had hidden some unused detonator caps in a false ceiling in a corner of Brett's room until he could retrieve and destroy them later. Jesse's bedroom ceiling in their old house didn't have any broken tiles that could be lifted, so he used Brett's room. All this circumstantial evidence seemed to have ruined a young man's life. Happily, Mitch's life was changed but not ruined. How do I know this?

Chapter Nine:
Yellow Roses Delivered

O n the evening of August 31st, a few days after I had heard that earth shattering news report, the buzzer on the outer door of my condo beeped. I had a delivery of some flowers. Could I come down to pick it up?—August 31st; could it possibly be?—Could it possibly be what I was thinking; flowers from Mitch? That was a pretty "way out there" thought. But it had been seven years.

I said I'd be right down, threw on a sweater, and grabbed my wallet for the tip. As I walked toward the door my heart was beating like I was running a race. Silly to be so affected by the thought of flowers. But these could be special flowers. I could think of no one else who would be sending me flowers. And the date of August 31st was right. I made my way to the door. I looked through the glass and stopped short. My mind could not take in what I was seeing. Looking back at me through the glass were the same clear hazel eyes, with eyelashes any girl would envy, and the same sandy hair that fell to one side above a strong angular face. It was Mitch. And he was still so handsome he still took my breath away. There was that same great smile I had so often seen smiling at me in my dreams. It was Mitch.

I fumbled with the lock, opened the door and stood frozen.

"Are you going to invite me in?", Mitch asked in that well- remembered, smooth, deep, voice.

I was speechless. When I regained my voice, I stammered , "Mitch is it really you?"

" Yes." He replied. "Although, the name I've been using for years is William Blakely, being called Will for short.

A thought crossed my mind, "Shades of the past". Robert called Rob. Now William called Will. I was hoping having another abbreviated name come into my life was not a bad omen.

Mitch continued saying, " The name I was born with is Brett Fairmore. And for a month now I have actually been able to answer to that name. It's a very long story and if you invite me in I'd like to share it with you."

I moved aside and without saying anything Mitch followed me to my condo. I really was in shock. After closing the door I took a seat by the large living room window in an antique whicker chair with soft blue floral cushions. Mitch sat in the formal dark blue velvet upholstered wing chair facing me.

As Mitch started to speak I quietly interrupted saying." I do know a little of the story. I was at the lake when I heard how you had been vindicated. And I saw your picture in the newspapers receiving an apology from the governor of Wyoming. I did look up some of the newspaper articles. But, I would very much like to hear the whole story."

I hugged my sweater around me and waited for Mitch to begin. Then Mitch in that voice I remembered so well, and had so often heard in my dreams, let me into his life in the years we had been apart.

Chapter Ten:
Mitch's Story

Mitch began, "The year I turned eighteen something really disastrous happened. As you have already heard, in Wyoming I was suspected of participating in a terrorist style bombing protest against the war in Vietnam and the conscription of young men at age eighteen. The bombing had injured ten workers at a munitions plant and resulted in the death of one of the bombers. My twenty-one year old brother Jesse had died when the bomb he was setting off detonated prematurely. The bombing had happened in the late evening when my brother and his friends assumed the factory would be empty, except for the two night watchmen, whom they could easily overpower and remove from the scene. The group had done their research and knew the factory would be shut up tight for the night. Only it wasn't. A meeting had been called for a skeleton crew to come in and make up lost production time because of a mechanical problem that day. As my brother and his friends were not professionals things did not go smoothly. The bomb detonated prematurely, simultaneously with them realizing the building was not empty. They had felt the munitions factory was the perfect place to show their anger at the Vietnam War and the conscription law which forced young men to be sent to die in the jungles of Vietnam. No one would get hurt and they could make a statement. It didn't turn out that way. Evidence found in our home implicated Jesse, his three friends and co-conspirators, and me. I was implicated as I had dropped my brother and his friends off near the bomb site. We were all facing criminal charges. I disappeared in the early morning darkness the morning after Jesse was killed. I then surfaced in Canada several months later as Mitchell Travers, only to once more disappear just before the RCMP closed in to make an arrest." said Mitch.

I had no involvement in the bombing. I had no knowledge of what my brother's group was planning when I dropped them off that night.

As conscription was looming for me I had previously made plans to "dodge the draft" and leave for Canada. I was scheduled to leave two days after dropping Jesse off with his friends. Obviously after what happened to Jesse that departure date was moved up.

When I turned eighteen I had been temporarily excluded from enlistment in the military draft because I was attending college. However, my exclusion had been cancelled because of some bureaucratic government mistake when I turned nineteen. I had submitted my second year college application in plenty of time but it had never been processed because of some bureaucratic slip-up. My parents had tried every avenue available to them to get the mistake corrected, but to no avail. Once the wheels of the U. S. military start turning nothing can stop them. I was to report to the enlistment office at the end of the week. I had discussed my options with my parents and it was agreed that leaving the country and heading to Canada to wait out the war was the best option for me. My family believed the war in Vietnam could not be won. They did not want their son's blood to be spilled on foreign soil for a futile war they felt should never have been started. A war that could not possibly end in victory for the United States. I had their blessing to run. My parents would rather see me disappear for as long as necessary rather than end up losing another son because of the war.

I had a stash of Canadian money, my escape route planned, and my minimal bag packed. I had been planning on savouring these last few days with my family to the fullest. With Jesse's death my departure schedule was moved up. That heartbreaking event gave me added incentive to leave. And to leave quickly. If someone had reported seeing a red Chevy drop off Jesse and his friends I would likely be considered a suspect. I didn't wait to find out. My plan was to find an out-of-the way place to work and wait out the war. Some place where it would be unlikely the long arm of the U. S. military and the U. S. justice system would reach me. I thought a small lake community in Canada near a small town would be the perfect place to remain out of sight and unnoticed. In retrospect it might have been better to have chosen to live in a big city, and try to get lost in the crowd. I made the wrong choice. But I have no regrets. If I hadn't come to the lake I wouldn't have met you. Besides the wonder of meeting you, in the long term it was a good choice. After the RCMP officers showed up at the Hall that night looking for me, I crept around to my room at the back of Eddie's store. I grabbed my "go bag" from the closet and made my way to ranch country in the beautiful foothills of Alberta and built a future.

In the seven years after I left you my life did change. I found a job on a ranch working for an old man named John Henry Cooper. Everyone called him Coop. He had put a "Help Wanted" ad for a ranch hand in the window of a small local diner in a town I was passing through. I hitched a ride out to his ranch. Coop was an older man who was sinewy, moved slowly, and was definitely past his prime. The job included a small "worse for wear" one bedroom house and three meals a day. The meals were cooked by a thin, little, also sinewy lady, named Alice. Alice came in once a week to cook meals for the freezer and once a week to clean and polish up Coop's place.

At the ranch I spent my time working with Coop learning to become an expert ranch hand. I made friends and built ties within the small ranching community. At this time my face was well-hidden under a beard, moustache, and square black glasses. I was cocooned from my fears of discovery, by the friendship shown to me by the community, as well as by the great distance that separated me from the long arm of U. S. military justice. I had found a safe haven, although the security I had found often felt tentative, as I was still considered a terrorist. That fact was never far from my mind.

A few years after I had stopped to read that "Help Wanted" ad in the town diner window, the owner named Belinda, became someone special in my life. Belinda was lovely to look at and a lovely person to know. Through my work on the ranch I had become a very adept, seasoned rider. As it turned out Belinda was more than a diner owner. She was an avid horsewoman. She was well- known through-out the area for winning rodeo competitions as a barrel racer and also winning ribbons in formal equestrian competitions. Eventually I became competent enough as a rider to participate in some of the local rodeos. I entered the individual Tie Down roping events and then the Team Roping events with my friend Samuel, our neighbour on the ranch adjacent to Coop's. Surprisingly I had some success and I came back to the ranch with a few ribbons. Back in Wyoming I was a city boy. I had never been to a rodeo, although Wyoming would certainly be considered cowboy country. A rodeo was out of the realm of anything I might have attended. But I was hooked from the first time I went with Coop. And I was hooked the first time I saw Belinda. Gradually after many drop-ins at the diner Belinda and I became a couple. As it turned out Belinda wasn't a fan of facial hair. So, it didn't take me long to get rid of it and soon the glasses I didn't need went as well.

Our life was great together. I had found a wonderful person to connect with. Our free time was spent out on day trips with a picnic lunch, riding across the grasslands filled with cattle, to the blue shade of the foothills. We went to rodeos together, and joined in the many community events which were always going on. I was doing things I had never done before; like enjoying a country fair and watching a pie-eating contest and a Barbecue Bake Off. There were barn dances and a weekly free movie night at the old single screen movie theatre in town. There was a community ice rink where you could be involved in, or just watch, curling or hockey. I was a specta-tor at those events and really enjoyed being part of the crowd. As I didn't skate I never tried hockey but I sure enjoyed watching it. Something really special was the community Christmas program with community members of all ages participating. Belinda even talked me into being a Wiseman, although the beard I had this time was fake. Belinda was the innkeeper's wife. I was very surprised that it was actually a lot of fun. So, my life was not only full and busy with everything to do with the ranch, but also the many events the small close-knit community provided. Something that was really exciting, was that I was starting to build a small house on the ranch to replace the old original place I was living in.

Although I was with Belinda and happy, there were many times you crossed my mind. And although amnesty for draft dodgers had been declared in the U. S. I was still stuck in limbo. I was still listed on a criminal watch list as a terrorist. So, I felt there was no way I could have come to you. Because I thought of you often didn't in any way diminish what I felt for Belinda. You were a distant dream and Belinda was loving and right beside me. Times were good.

What Belinda and I shared came unexpectedly and suddenly to an abrupt end. She was originally from Wyoming which was some-thing that had brought us together when we first met. Belinda was a country girl who grew up on a huge ranch in Wyoming. I was a city boy who was becoming an Alberta rancher. We found common ground in our love of horses and being out enjoying the beautiful ranch country surrounding us. Belinda had never planned on living in a small town, far from Wyoming, owning a diner. But her father had become ill and her father's older brother along with his family, had come to run the ranch. It was a bad situation. Her uncle was running the ranch into the ground. And there was no place for Belinda in her uncle's plan. So, she left and made a new life far away, but still somewhere, where there was ranch country and horses.

Our life together was over when Belinda's father died. His will left everything to her. Belinda returned to Wyoming. There was no way I could return to Wyoming as there I was still a wanted criminal. Plus, I had built a life I loved in Canada and I had no wish to leave. So with sad feelings but great fondness we split up. And life moved on.

A few months after Belinda left, one day near the date of August 31st, I realized on that date it would be exactly seven years since I had left you. Ever since we had heard your grandmother's saying about life changing every seven years the thought sometimes crossed my mind. Wondering could it be true? You and I had laughed at all her "Old Wives Tales" sayings and she did say them with a smile on her face and a twinkle in her eye. But the saying about change happening every seven years she actually did believe. So we paid it more attention.

So far her saying had proven to be true. My life had changed after seven years. I was moving on without Belinda. Maybe I could make another change as well. I had thought of you so often suddenly I had this perhaps unrealistic idea that I should take the risk and come to see you. A friend who published the local newspaper in town used his contacts to find your information. He had found out where you worked, your address, and that you were single. I'm sure he broke some privacy rules to get the information. I was still considered a terrorist but I had been living a life safely in Canada despite that. Maybe you and I could do the same together. I hoped you remembered me with the same intensity of affection I remembered you. I made my plans. I had my truck packed

The night before I was planning to leave to come find you, a tornado swept through the Alberta foothills, its wrath wreaking terrible havoc. Coop's ranch was directly in its path. There wasn't much left of his old house, my new house, the barns and all the outbuildings except what looked like sticks of kindling big and small. Coop was hurt badly trying to get the horses out of the barn quickly as soon as we heard the tornado warning. He would need care, someone to run the ranch, and orchestrate the rebuilding. That person would have to be me. Even in the chaos surrounding the tornado I still wanted to let you to know I remembered you and thought of you often. So, I went into town wired the roses and the note, then got totally involved in the massive project of rebuilding the ranch.

As time passed and the years added up I was conscious every so often of your grandmother's seven year time frame and that it would soon again be reached. In my time on the ranch I became an expert ranch hand. There was nothing on the ranch I couldn't do or couldn't fix. I learned the cattle business and also how to manage the small area of crop land Coop had. But most enjoyably I developed a deep love of horses. I spent time raising them, training them, and being around them constantly on the ranch. Riding in the wide open spaces of the ranch land became a favourite pastime, as well as competing in local rodeo competitions.

After Belinda I did have someone else in my life for awhile. She was an insurance appraiser for the county and I originally met her when she came out to the ranch to appraise the tornado damage. She didn't enjoy country living. Her heart was in the city. She had "escaped" ranch country for the bright city lights when she was eighteen. She had only returned to ranch country to financially help her family. When her family had to sell the ranch because of financial difficulties I was not enough to hold her. She very quickly left ranch country for a return once again to the excitement of the big city. We had enjoyed each other but not enough to make a life together. We parted as very good friends.

In the years after the tornado struck besides being busy with re-building the ranch I was enjoying being involved with the community. Coop was in failing health so he had made me part owner of the ranch with the intention that when he was gone the ranch would come to me. He had no family so it would not be a problem to hand it over to me. One day when I was mending fence lines out on the range it came to me that another seven years had crept up again since I had left you. They had been a busy seven years. As August 31st approached and I still so often thought of you I decided it was time to try again to see you. Past time. You really were my first love. Besides some very unusual events keeping us apart and life moving on, I thought possibly you were why the "spark" was never quite as strong with anyone else. Was it because of you? It was time to find out.

My plan was to deliver roses to you at the end of August. It was just a coincidence about the seven years, although maybe a hidden thought about your grandmother's saying was somewhere in the back of my mind. But the date of Aug 31st I chose. I set up my trip so I would be at your door on August 31st. I was looking forward to knocking on your door and hopefully seeing you smile when you opened it.

My truck was packed. I had once again enlisted the help of my publisher friend to find information on you, to make sure I wasn't going on a wild goose chase and that you were still single. - You were. Although in my mind that was hard to believe.

I was ready to leave when I heard Coop yell from the barn. Coop was a very early riser. As he got older he didn't sleep well. He was still doing things around the ranch that he shouldn't have been doing because of his age and poor health. That morning he had been forking hay from the hay loft for the horses below when he caught his foot on a coiled rope hidden under the hay. Coop fell from the hayloft to the floor cracking the back of his head wide open and seriously injuring his back. My planned trip to see you was put on hold once more. Coop did partially recover. His head healed with his mind intact. But his back and one leg were never quite right again. I took over managing the ranch. Because of Coop's accident he passed the ranch ownership and responsibility on to me. I went into town and once more wired yellow roses and a note. My life had changed again.

The next seven years crept up on me and passed quickly with both challenges and successes. Coop passed away leaving me the ranch and the necessity of finding and training a new and trusted right hand man. A local kid named Wes fit the bill. Together we enlarged the ranch and used new techniques to improve our herd of black angus cattle as well as increase the yield of our crops. I was still doing some raising and training of horses. I was constantly busy but I wasn't a kid anymore. I was slowly becoming more aware of the passing of time. I had no "significant other" and I thought of you very often, wondering what our life might have been like if there had been no war, no bomb hurriedly detonated, no need to avoid conscription into the military, and no concern about being arrested. We were so good together I just knew we could have filled our lives with a strong enduring love. I made up my mind. And with great purpose set out to find out if you were still single. Actually, I got my lawyer to do it. Going through legal channels he was successful-You were. I was sure there had been loves in your life but it was my good fortune that there was no one in your life right now. I made my plans. I would be at your door on August 31 with a large bouquet of yellow roses.

Happily, what coincided with my trip to see you was that I was cleared of all criminal charges. Then I really was free to come find you. So here I am. And you are even more beautiful than my memories could ever have portrayed." Mitch said softly.

He asked, "Do you think we might spend time together and find out if what we shared at the lake that summer is still strong? That was the best summer of my life. And it was all because of you."

I didn't answer for a moment. I just drank him in with my eyes. That he was here sitting across from me was just so unreal.

Then I replied. " I've never forgotten that summer. I've never forgotten you. Fate and circumstances beyond our control shaped our lives then. I'm so very willing to have us shape our future together now. Shape it the way it should have gone that summer."

When I finished speaking Mitch stood up. He stepped toward me. He took my hand and he pulled me into his arms. It was wonderful, impossible, and wonderful, and heavenly. My story could be told at a later time. With that first kiss the hands of time moved backwards. We were seventeen and nineteen again in the summer at the lake.

Chapter Eleven:
I Became a Rancher

Mitch stayed with me for a month. I took time off from my job and we were together constantly. At the end of a month together we knew it was right. Just as we had known that summer at the lake. Mitch had to get back to the ranch. I quit my job, packed up, and followed him a month later. I was a city girl but with Mitch by my side I became a rancher. And I loved it. I loved the beauty of the land, the animals, especially the horses, and the hot burning flame of love that Mitch and I shared. Life had changed again.

In the next seven years there were many changes. When I arrived at the ranch it didn't take long for me to be accepted and welcomed by Mitch's friends and associates. As Mitch was well-known, liked, and highly respected I had an immediate "in" within the ranching community. As I accompanied Mitch to rodeos, pot lucks and horse sales I gradually became accepted on my own merit. After some months I decided I wanted to be involved in doing something on my own. To make my own mark in the community. After all, I had been an independent woman forging my own path in my previous life. My life was full working with Mitch on the ranch and I loved it. And

I loved being with him, but I felt like I wanted to spread my wings a little with a project of my own.

One day in town I found the perfect solution to my quest for my independent venture. I stopped in at the town library. I had always considered libraries very special places. They were quiet, calm spaces. The buildings were always bright and pleasant. And where else can you browse, "shop", and come home with a "treasure", without spending any money. For such a small town it had a huge old library. The building was from the early nineteen hundreds and the architecture was amazing. There were huge multi-paned windows filling the place with light. The dark ornately carved wood accents were highly polished as were the solid wood floors. Around every corner there was a delight; be it a window seat tucked into an alcove, or an area separated by gorgeous frosted glass panels etched with depictions of local flowers. There were comfortable high backed, well padded, chocolate brown leather chairs to sink into. And where there was an alcove or a cluster of chairs the area was defined beautifully by brightly coloured, elegant carpets. The place was gorgeous. And it was obviously well used, as was demonstrated by a group of visiting students and their teacher. I could see they were learning to do animation on high end computers in one of the rooms adjoining the main area.

There was a bulletin board in the front foyer of the library with a note tacked to it asking for a volunteer willing to teach art classes. As that was right up my alley, and as I had always loved spending time in libraries, I signed up immediately. I was given a junior group and senior group to work with. The kids were great and through them I developed friendly relationships with their parents. Through teaching the art classes as well as helping with the community pot lucks I found two good friends. One was a petite, slim, black woman who was absolutely stunning. Her name was Louella and she was originally from Alabama. She still had the soft Alabama accent from her home state. Louella's husband William, had a friend in college who was from Alabama. And when William was staying with this friend on a school holiday, William met Louella. It was love at first sight. And the rest is history. Louella became a proud Albertan. Louella's teenage daughter was in my senior group and was very talented. Her paintings were fantastic.

The second special person who became a good friend was Shailene. And in complete contrast to Louella, Shailene was a tall, buxom, blonde with big hair and a big laugh. Her teenage daughter was also in my senior group and was also a gifted artist. Both mothers had been friends forever. And both daughters were friends. It was lovely that I became part of that special little circle.

Because the art classes were going so well, and because there seemed to be such a wealth of talent in both age groups it was decided we should have an art show and sale at the library. Louella and Shailene helped me organize it. Their two girls were definitely the mainstay of talent in the show. In the first hour of the show both girls received offers to display their art for sale in the gift shop on the town's main street. They were "over the moon" about that. As it was known I was an artist I was also asked to display my work. I didn't really have much to display as I previously sold my work. But I did have a few pieces and they were snatched up right away to be sold in the same gift shop as Louella and Shailene's daughters. Like the girls I was pretty "over the moon" about that too.

The art show was fun. And it was satisfying to see my work once again displayed and valued. I had put my art away being busy on the ranch. But maybe in the future I would get back to it. The art show absolutely bonded the friendship between me and Louella and Shailene. It was great.

A big change that came along a year and a half after I moved to the ranch was that Mitch and I were gifted with twins, Blake Jonathan Travers and Serena Rose Travers. It seems sometimes fate works in strange ways. My sadness at Rob not wanting to have children, and the loss of Danny before that could happen for us, had paved the way for my over the top, absolutely limitless joy, of having Blake and Serena. They were such wonderful treasures to be given and were perfectly timed for the start of a new life.

And added to the gift of these small wonders was another gift after the babies were born-in the form of Louella and Shailene. These two women who had become my good friends turned out to be two would-be angels. Every morning for the first months after the twins were born, one, or sometimes both, showed up on our doorstep to efficiently and lovingly help me get the twins ready for the day. A bond and circle of caring flowed from them to Blake and Serena, and to me, which I then returned to them. Louella and Shailene pretty much adopted two pampered and much loved babies as their own. As time went on Louella and Shailene came less in the mornings but often stopped by supposedly for coffee in the afternoon. Funny thing was, as soon as they saw the twins they had one on each knee. These smiling women would talk to Blake and Serena in a matter of fact manner, telling them about events of their day and then telling Blake and Serena how much they'd missed them. Of course these two babies had no understanding of what was being said but the gentle chatter, and the love being directed at them in full force, brought big, bright-eyed smiles to their faces.

As Mitch and I had no family close by, the helping hands and love shown by these two special women was something for which we would be forever grateful.

As the twins got older I was stepping into deeper involvement in the raising, training, and then selling to respected buyers, the horses we raised. I started to be involved in that part of the ranch business. And Mitch was all for it. Expanding the ranch business more fully into raising horses suited him just fine!

Most afternoons, first in the two-seat stroller and then as they got older on the viewing benches outside the corral fence, Blake and Serena would sit and be entertained. They would watch what was going on as either Mitch or I, was inside the corral working with one of the horses. For someone who had never been near horses I fell in love with them. I grew to appreciate their beauty as well as their intelligence and in most cases their gentle, loyal nature. I never became a proficient enough, or a confident enough rider, to try rodeo sports like barrel racing or even to participate in equestrian events or formal dressage events. I was perfectly happy to be on the other end of the spectrum using my accounting and business skills to keep the ranch doing well financially. But it so enriched my life to also be part of the raising and training of these beautiful animals along with Mitch. It was such a pleasure to be doing something we loved and doing it together side by side. I enjoyed working with the horses from their birth to their selling. There were some that tugged at your heart more than others but the business of raising hoses was becoming a large part of our ranch operation. So, there was no way every loveable animal could be kept.

Until one day there was an exception. A newborn colt made his way completely into my heart. He was jet black with a little white star on his forehead. I helped train him and he was perfect. He was the smartest, sweetest little guy. I named him Star and we became a team for pleasure riding and for simple ranch chores like checking fence lines for fallen fence sections or riding across the expansive grasslands to check for cattle who might have wondered off. Work and pleasure combined. What could be better? Mitch had a big black stallion called Midnight. Midnight and Star were buddies. They were a mismatched pair for sure. Midnight was very large, tall and power-ful, whereas Star was a medium to smaller height quarter horse of much lighter build. They were often seen standing close together at the fence in the pasture, their necks resting on one another. They thought they were brothers!

Mitch often entered Midnight in the races held at local fairs. Midnight was not only big and magnificent to look at. He was fast, really fast. As was proven by the many ribbons he won. Watching

Midnight race became a family affair. Being a part of the " racing for fun" community added another happy dimension to our ranch life.

I'm sure in the coming years we'll have two more ranchers in the ranch business. Serena and Blake love to sit in front of us on our saddles as we are out riding across the huge expanse of ranch land that will eventually be theirs. Before bed Blake and Serena like to be taken to the warm, dusty, stables filled with the smell of dried hay, feed, and oats, to see the horses. They like to touch the prickly bales of the hay used to line the floors of the stable stalls. The quiet of the stables and the horses within on a quiet pre-bedtime stroll, is a favourite way to settle Blake and Serena in for the night. Before we leave the stables the last thing Blake and Serena especially like to do is reach out from their secure spots in Mitch and my arms, to gently touch the satiny smooth noses of Star and Midnight.

My grandmother's saying had proven to be true. For Mitch and I our lives had changed in seven year increments, " sometimes for better", "sometimes for worse".

During the seven year increment we are now working on, there have been many changes. In this case the changes I've described have all been changes " for better". And Mitch and I believe in our hearts when this seven year time frame ends the changes in the next seven years will also be of the " for better" variety.

In the evenings after Serena and Blake are tucked in for the night Mitch and I sit very close together on the porch swing on our veran-dah. We enjoy seeing the blue twilight settling over the distant foot-hills. As we sit in the soft silence we can hear the night animals near and far going about their nightly chores. And as I look up at a sky starting to fill with brilliant stars I like to think that my grandmother might be smiling down on us, her eyes twinkling at how her seven year theory had proven to be true.

The war in Vietnam did influence the way my life unfolded. Which is surprising because as I said at the beginning of my story " If you lived on the Canadian prairies in the 1960's as I did, you were about as far removed from the Vietnam war with the United States as it was possible to be." Yet the far reaching arm of the Vietnam war did touch me.

The Vietnam war lasted from 1955 to 1975 and after thousands of deaths and untold broken lives and broken bodies, it did prove to be a war that the United states could not win.

BOOK TWO

I Don't Remember

BOOK TWO

I DON'T REMEMBER

Table of Contents

Chapter One:
A Very Bad Day

E ver wake up with amnesia? Well I have. And it's a horrify-ing experience.

My name is Seraphina Douglas, or so I'm told. I seem to be 5'8" tall, with red hair and green eyes. I'm twenty-six years old. All that information is under the picture on my new driver's licence. There are so many strange things about my amnesia. I can remember how to drive and read. I'm excellent at math and accounting. I can remember how to assess a property either for development or sale. Which means I can continue to work in my "father's" office as a land agent. I have a certificate on my office wall showing that I have a degree in Economics. I really do not feel like a Seraphina.

I'm trying to fit back into my old life. I'm trying to be ordinary. I'm trying not to be that woman who can't remember who she is. I'm so tired of the inquiring looks and the quiet whispers after I pass by. I'm trying to make some kind of a connection with this cold, austere man I work for. And who apparently is my father. I'm trying to get to know my annoying younger sister with her "snobby" attitude toward anyone who isn't in her social strata. I'm sure she must have always been annoying. I see pictures of my deceased mother, whom I very much resemble, and I feel deeply sad that I have no recollection of how she loved me. There are pictures of her with me as a child. And you can see by our smiles the love wrapped around us. I do not remember knowing her or loving her.

There is one bright spot in my unsettled, unexplained life. And that is my mother's mother. It is my warm, funny grandmother who I guess I have always called Gran. She is loving, caring, and irreverent. She says what she thinks with no apologies, but always with the best interest at heart, of the person she is "tuning up". No matter what the situation you know she is always on your side with support and love. It was Gran who got me back to a semi-normal life. With her laughter and advice she helped me find the steps to build a new life, to quit grieving what was lost, and to move forward.

I made a decision. After some heart to heart talks with Gran, I moved out of my father's house. I had been there since the accident. I went back to my condo. It was like moving to a totally new space. I was surrounded by things I should have remembered and that should have been comforting. But, I had absolutely no connection to any of them. After a few months, following Gran's advice, I put everything into storage and started fresh. I could not live in hope, thinking my memory would return in a sudden flash of remembrance. I packed everything. And I mean everything. All that was left was a totally empty shell. I picked out new paint, new drapes, new linens, new housewares, new décor items, rugs, everything. Oh, I didn't throw out any of the things I removed and packed away. They were safely stored so that if some day I remembered, they would be there for me, to help me reclaim my past.

I continued to work in my father's office for a year. Then I took a leave of absence and took a trip. If I was being honest, as Gran suggested I should be, I wasn't doing well living my old life, one that was so full of holes. It was time to build a new life with the new me. Make some new memories with some new people who didn't know the previous me. When I landed somewhere new I decided I would use my middle name Anne(Annie) and my last name would be Smith. With two such common names maybe I could melt into my new life with no past attached to me. The name Seraphina Douglas was too recognizable to start a new life with. That name had too much baggage, and too much notoriety, from being in the news so much. Plus, I was finding I really wasn't enjoying being in the top 1% of the upper strata of society. I wanted something different. Something with less artifice and more substance. Don't get me wrong. I wasn't totally embracing lower class living. I couldn't give up my expensive wardrobe which included the shoes, purses, and coats I loved. Although I wouldn't know or remember, I guess I had never been much for jewellery. So, I put the pieces I did have in my safety deposit box in case I ever wanted them. That was unlikely to happen. I didn't remember any of the pieces as keepsakes from certain people, or as gifts for special events, or as gifts to mark milestones in my life. Though, to my new life I did take one piece of jewellery, a thin gold bangle bracelet from Gran, given to me after the accident, and a small gold locket with a picture of my mother and me. I didn't remember the picture or her but I could feel the love she had for me shining out through the photo. I wasn't sure what I wanted to do. But I definitely wanted a different type of life.

Although I was moving on to try start a new life I was still often terrified about what had been, why it happened to me, and what was to come. Especially at night bad dreams would come, bringing memories just out of reach, of sudden and terrible pain. Then just as suddenly a black curtain with tiny ruffled edges of memory trying to creep through, would be drawn across my dreamscape and I would wake up shivering.

Chapter Two:
What Happened?

Hearing about these ongoing problems and my memory's response to the trauma of the accident you might ask, "How did she get into this life altering situation "?

Well, these are the details of my near deadly crash—which I found out about much later from the people involved. As well—this is my own recounting of the events following the accident, as I know them, and also my recounting of how my life moved forward, after the crash.

Two years ago, on September 5, 1960, I was found unconscious laying half in and half out of an easement on a rural gravel road. I had a huge goose egg and multicoloured bruise across half of my forehead. I had a deep gash across the back of my head, just above my neck, which was bleeding profusely. Near where I lay the debris of smashed window glass, pieces of a red tail light, and pieces of a silver metal bumper made it apparent that my car had been rammed from behind by a much larger vehicle. The impact likely caused my driver's door to fly open and I was tossed out into the easement. Seemingly with no humanity in their soul, someone left me there bleeding, then drove away with my car, followed by the larger vehicle.

Of course I have no recollection of these events. This was what I was told. Because my purse was in my car I was left among the road grass, gravel, and weeds with no ID, no money, and no memory.

Luckily for me a man on his way to town saw a swatch of bright pink at the edge of that rough, narrow road. The bright pink he saw was part of a bright pink suit jacket, with only the sleeve that had caught his attention, being free of blood. The rest of the jacket had been flooded with bright red and the area around the back collar was so saturated it was starting to darken ominously. I later learned the man's name was Nate Kendall. And from him much later I heard the details of how he found me and saved me.

Nate had some paramedical training in a previous life. I was unconscious but he found a pulse and packed my neck tightly with his jacket to stop the bleeding. Then he checked for other injuries to be sure I could be moved. As he checked my arms and legs I started mumbling which he took as a good sign. Then he lifted me on to a clean tarp in the box of his truck and carefully and slowly started down the long barely discernible overgrown path which led into a tree line of firs and aspens. He continued on even deeper into a green wall of branches and tree trunks until he arrived at a very small, very worn, old log cabin. It was partially hidden by a veil of tall growing brambles.

What I didn't know, and didn't find out until many months later, was that Nate Kendall was an undercover DEA (Drug Enforcement Agent) who had run into a big problem with a huge drug bust and had to disappear. His cover had been blown and he was laying low, very low, until this particularly vicious group of drug dealers was caught.

It was much too dangerous for him to take me into the town to the hospital in daylight. So, he cared for me in the log cabin during the day. That night, when nature was in agreement, and there was no moonlight, he carefully loaded me and my expensive blood soaked jacket into the truck. He then headed down the overgrown path, out of the forest, and onto the skinny gravel road which led to the tiniest hospital, in the tiniest town, my big-city eyes had ever seen, when I finally regained consciousness.

The hospital notified the sheriff of my surprise arrival. As I had no ID the sheriff started looking through postings and notices of anyone who had been reported missing in the hours before I was left anonymously at the hospital. My description wasn't on any list. The label in my jacket helped in discovering my identity. The jacket was made by a famous designer who designed for only a select clientele. The morning after I arrived at the hospital the designer was contacted and he gave the sheriff my name. Not long after that my name also came up in the missing person data base showing my father had contacted the police. When the police researched my last name and the information showed I was extremely wealthy, an immediate concern was kidnapping.

After a lengthy discussion among themselves the small town police force discarded that idea. As I was unknown in their small community, and the type of injuries I had sustained definitely pointed to a car crash, they felt it was unlikely I had been injured in a kidnapping attempt. Their analysis of the incident was that it was a carjacking gone wrong. Lately there had been a gang in the area stealing vehicles. This same gang had been involved in several carjackings on country roads in the last few months.

However, there was a mystery attached to my story. How did I get to the hospital? The police knew I couldn't have made it to the hospital on my own. So, how did I get there? As their conclusion was that I had been in a serious vehicle collision, they set about finding the scene of the crash. When they found the crash site they felt their conclusion was correct. What had caused my accident was definitely a carjacking, not an attempted kidnapping.

When I finally regained consciousness three days after I had turned up on the doorstep of the hospital, a tall, distinguished looking man with hair greying at the temples, was standing at the foot of my bed. He was looking down at me with riveted attention. Creepy! Who the heck was this weirdo staring at me while I was sleeping? I started hollering for the nurse and the man came even closer. With terrible panic in my voice and my heart, I kept yelling for the nurse. The grey-haired man just stood very calmly looking down at me. He didn't say a word.

A little nurse who couldn't possibly have moved any faster, came rushing at full speed into the room. She came to my bed and took my hand.

" Seraphina, Seraphina, Seraphina, this is your father", she kept repeating soothingly.

All I could think was, " Who is she talking too? Who is Seraphina?"

The little nurse continued, "This is your father. He's come to take you home. He and your sister have come to take you home. Don't be afraid. You were hurt in an accident. Sometimes the kind of head injuries you received cause temporary amnesia."

I'm thinking, " 'temporary amnesia'. That's not even a real thing. That's what you read about in novels. This must be a nightmare. I don't feel like a Seraphina. And I don't want to know this man."

The little nurse turned to the tall distinguished-looking man with the cold grey eyes and the hard uncompromising expression saying, "Mr. Douglas I think you had better leave until Seraphina speaks with the doctor. If you would just go back to the waiting room I think that would be better for now. You can speak with Seraphina after the doctor sees her."

And with that she quickly turned back to me, smiling at me, speaking softly, and gently holding my hand. Being dismissed, Thomas Douglas angrily strode into the waiting room to explain to his daughter Francine, the ridiculous reason she couldn't see her sister. That ridiculous reason being that Seraphina supposedly had amnesia. Which to the mind of the important Mr. Thomas Douglas was absolute poppycock!

After my "supposed" father left the doctor did come to see me. He explained that I had a head injury and that I could possibly have some temporary memory problems for awhile. He said I was dropped off at the hospital by an unknown person late at night. So, no one actually knew what had happened to me, but it was assumed my injuries were caused by a vehicle collision in a possible carjacking. I couldn't believe I wouldn't remember being in a possible carjacking. I started thinking I was in serious trouble.

I was in the hospital for a month while my injuries healed. Periodically a hospital psychiatrist would come and try to help me remove the dead end roadblock which seemed to have stopped my memory cold. Nothing worked. Finally I was allowed to go home with the austere grey-haired man and my cold, unfriendly "supposed" sister I couldn't remember— to the life I also couldn't remember. After a year when finding I could not adjust to my old life I decided to build a new life.

Chapter Three:
A New Life

When I left my father's home and my father's firm to start my new life as Annie Smith I moved to a small city called Wiseboro, three towns away from the area where the accident had happened. In some respects that might not have been smart, but it was as if a magnet was drawing me to the area. I couldn't seem to help myself. Maybe subconsciously I hoped being near the site of the crash might trigger my memory. When the police had found the crash site they definitely settled on the theory my crash was caused by an attempted carjacking gone wrong. The tire tracks at the scene showed evidence of one very large, heavy vehicle, probably an oversized truck, and a much smaller vehicle. Their thinking was that if I had perceived I was in danger on a lonely, empty road with a huge truck bearing down on me I may have sped up to escape trouble. If both vehicles were travelling at high speeds in a chase, a collision would have been very powerful, propelling my smaller vehicle into the easement. While my car was being propelled forward it was probable my door flew open and I was torpedoed out. At least that was the most likely scenario the police could come up with to explain how I had been found in the easement. The group of thieves involved in the carjackings had been targeting smaller communities with smaller police forces, where there was less chance of capture. According to the local police I was just an unlucky victim. That could be true as I was driving the most expensive high end car on the market. That car could bring in a lot of money if sold.

It was quite a coincidence though, that I was alone and unexpectedly driving myself to a meeting which left me very unprotected. I was assessing a large, rich, rural property for my father's company. That property was part of an ugly family dispute. My father's company had been given several nasty warnings by the family saying that if the assessment didn't go the way this one particular side of the family wanted, there would be serious consequences. The family had been told by the police to cease and desist with those messages or there would be charges laid. Though the messages did stop my father's company wasn't taking any chances. That's why I wasn't going alone on to the property. I was to meet a local assessor and we would check out the property together. Because of my complacency about no threats of kidnapping for years, and the fact I was to meet with the local assessor who would be acting as my security at the rural property, I was overly confident in my safety.

I certainly normally wouldn't have been driving out of the city by myself. But on this particular day our family was short staffed of our employees who doubled as bodyguards. My sister needed a driver and some of my father's associates who were in town for a meeting requested some protection as well. My family was so careful to fly under the radar and there had never been a kidnapping threat in the last forty years so I was not too concerned. I guess I had become too comfortable in my secure lifestyle. My feeling was that because we had been safe for so many years a short drive alone should be fine. And it was so wonderful to just take off on my own, driving myself and feeling the freedom of the road.

As extra security for me, the adjuster who was coming out to meet me to assess the land that was in dispute, was an ex-military marine police officer. He was to be my security as he and I did our assessment of the land. Because the two families whose parents had owned the land were bitterly contesting it's ownership, the ranch was the location where my father thought protection would be needed, not on the drive out to the ranch. Most of the drive to the ranch was on a busy highway with lots of traffic, lots of people around. It was only on the few miles of gravelled country road that I would be alone. As I said, complacency was my downfall which lead to disaster. I hadn't driven myself anywhere in so long I was looking at this job as a bit of an escape from the tight bonds of my protected existence. And oh, it felt good. That is until the assessor with protection skills I was to meet with didn't show, and couldn't be contacted. I made the correct decision and immediately turned back toward the main highway. Too late. The wheels were already in motion which ended with me in the hospital with no memory of my past.

So, disaster happened because of my over confidence, perhaps because of a crime of opportunity, and perhaps because of the unprofessional action of my missing ex- marine security guard. It was a case of everything going wrong that could go wrong. When the assessor didn't turn up at the meeting place my decision was that I wasn't going into that powder keg of a family dispute without protection. I had tried to contact the assessor on the drive to the appointment, pulling over to the side of the road and using the car phone to call his office. I had listened to a message saying he was out of the office meeting with a client. I assumed I was this "so called" client. So, I continued on to the meeting place which was the entrance to the ranch. The entrance was to be clearly marked by a large sign bearing the family name. What I didn't know was that the message I heard on the assessor's phone was his standard message for every set of circumstances. I found out later the office was closed that day for some kind of family celebration. It also came to light that his chirpy little secretary Earline had given him the wrong date for our meeting. I guess the assessor wasn't unprofessional, just blamelessly ignorant.

At the accident site my tracks showed I was heading away from the property. The police assumed I was turning around to go back to the main highway when my car was rammed. As time passed and my father hadn't heard from me with my land assessment report he did start to panic. Not particularly about my welfare. But about problems that could arise, and that would reflect on the family reputation, if I had gotten myself into some kind of trouble travelling without a bodyguard. He had seemingly forgotten he had okayed my drive with no bodyguard. He did report me as missing to the police about midnight. Yes, his concern was about a possible kidnapping. Though, for him more worrisome than concern for my well-being, was the thought of having to pay a huge ransom. My sister coldly informed me about the real reason for my father's fears when I came home from the hospital. My father was not a warm-hearted man. His heart was frozen solid. It was a cold, hard piece of ice. His concerns were his money, his reputation, and his social standing within the business world of extreme wealth. According to my equally cold-hearted sister the possibility of a kidnapping and a ransom trumped any worry about me. If I did come to harm it would be considered to be my own fault, because of my rash decision to travel alone. Which in all honesty, I did have to admit could be considered to be true. No matter what the circumstances there would be very little sympathy for me if, and when, I did turn up.

After I recovered, to me the carjacking theory really didn't make sense. Why would the thieves damage such an expensive vehicle when they could have gotten ahead of me and blocked my path. Of course that gave truth to the very disturbing thought that I was the target. And that disturbing thought played a large part in my decision to get away from my father's firm. Also included in that decision was the wish to get away from the father I didn't remember and certainly didn't love, and a sister who was definitely unlovable, emotionless, and very hard to be around. How could I have grown up with these people? And how had I avoided becoming like them?

After the accident when I had re-connected with Gran, I had asked her about my upbringing with such cold, uncaring people.

Gran said, "After your mother died you spent most of your time living with me. And when you were in your father's house, Edna as well as being your father's live-in housekeeper and cook, loved you like her own child. She was always watching out for you and caring for you. Your sister would not leave your father to come to my house. And even at a young age Francine didn't want to have anything to do with Edna because of what she considered Edna's lower social status. Consequently, that is why Francine became just like your father."

I then asked Gran how my mother, her child, could possibly have married such an unfeeling, overbearing man.

Gran answered, "Believe it or not, your father was quite charming when your mother met him. Sometimes the high opinion he had of himself did slip through, but mostly it was very well hidden. Unfortunately for your mother he could convincingly pass himself off as a caring, loving person when it suited his purpose."

Gran continued, "Your father just wanted a beautiful woman of equal social standing on his arm. Your mother was a prize he worked hard to achieve. The marriage became rocky soon after the wedding. And it got worse when you and Francine were born. You and Francine were just symbols of his success, just as my beautiful, intelligent, loving daughter was. Your mother was planning to take you and Francine and leave him. However, when she got sick and didn't recover, life changed."

Chapter Four:
A New Occupation

When I made the decision to leave my old life I distanced myself from everything I couldn't remember, with the exception of Gran, Edna, and Janey. Janey who had apparently been my life-long best friend. And who in my new life, had once again worked her way into my heart. Taking these few ties to my unknown past with me I moved on and started my new life as Annie Smith.

I wanted to do something entirely different. I had a secondary degree in journalism which made me decide to look into my options for a career in that area. I found out from acquaintances I didn't remember, and friends I didn't remember, that I had always been into good eating, and exercise. I did seem to be quite fit and I had actually liked working out in our home gym, swimming in our home pool, and eating healthy food choices. Gran told me how Edna took me under her wing and taught me how to cook healthy food. Gran also said that in my father's house Edna was the only one who had supported whatever I wanted to do.

After I started my new life the few times I returned to the city I slipped in the back entrance of my father's house to see Edna. Even with no previous memory of Edna I knew immediately she had been my ally in that huge empty shell of a house. After talking to Gran, the next time I stopped by to see Edna, I asked her to tell me more details of the times we had spent together. Edna said the first time I showed up in the kitchen wanting to cook it just brightened her day. She said that even at a young age I was interested in cooking and recipes. I suppose Edna being a motherly sort, and me a motherless child, I gravitated to her and the kitchen. Edna said at first she taught me to bake. Then when I was in high school I decided I should eat a healthier diet. Edna humoured me and taught me what she knew. It sounded like we had a lot of fun, with lots of smiles and laughter in that huge cathedral-like kitchen, trying new recipes with a healthy bias. Edna said when the recipes were done she and I would taste test the results of our investigative cooking adventures. We were pleased with our successes. My father and sister thought this was just a fad I was going through. My father thought it was ridiculous. And that this kind of extremely healthy cooking was a waste of time. I knew from experience with my father after my accident, that ridiculous was a term much overused by him- often in reference to me or my past activities. Edna said on principle, my father and sister wouldn't touch any of the new dishes she and I had made. When presented with our new recipes my father said he couldn't condone such fool-ishness by eating any part of such a meal. Which of course left Edna making a regular meal as well for my father and sister. My father said that Edna and I could surely find something better to do with our time. He said Edna in particular, should be concentrating more on the work she was paid to do. She should waste less time in the kitchen on silly activities with me. Edna told me both she and I ignored his comments on our so called silly activities. Edna, because she knew he would have a very tough time replacing her with someone who was satisfactory, and me, because I had grown to have no respect for anything my father said. As for my sister, after "turning up her nose" at what Edna and I had made, apparently Francine always had the same comment for me.

"What are you trying to be? A lower level cook like Edna? Or maybe you want to get a job flipping burgers at the Dairy Queen". Edna had developed a "thick skin" working for my father so she said any of Francine's miserable little comments never bothered her. For me, after hearing the absolute meanness of another of Francine's past comments it was just another reason, among so many, that helped validate my reasons to leave my father's home. It caused me no pain at all to remove myself from my sister's orbit!

One of the most difficult things of my memory loss, was not remembering acquaintances, relatives, or even a life-long best friend. Seeing pictures of Janey and I together, whether adorable, funny, or sad, could not connect me to this short, slim, angelic looking, little person with blonde curls and big blue eyes.

Although I didn't remember her, I was immediately drawn to her. Janey along with Gran helped weave me a tapestry depicting the people and events of my previous life. When I changed cities Janey and I still remained close through our old/new friendship. She came to visit. And when I went back to stay with Gran, Janey often stayed at Gran's with me. Janey was smart. She was a lawyer with a prestigious, high-end law firm. Her quick-witted sense of humour could be hilarious. I guess we had always laughed a lot. I loved it when she and Gran told me stories about my life. It was like opening a book full of surprises every time. And I always loved it when Gran told me about my mother. Those stories were golden. They made me feel anchored and grounded knowing I had been given a solid, loving, start in life.

The city of Wiseboro I chose for my new home, was a city chosen to be a capital city because of its location during the time of the railway. When railway traffic was no longer its main drawing point Wiseboro did not grow to the size that was expected. It remained one of the smallest capital cities in the country. I liked the smaller size: less busy traffic (only took twenty minutes to get across town most days when traffic was light), less frenzied shoppers out and about. This smaller city definitely had a much more relaxed atmosphere than the big city I was used too. These were all good reasons for Wiseboro to be the choice for my move. One of the biggest factors in my choice of Wiseboro was that I snagged a job at the Wiseboro Weekly, the local newspaper. I was hired as a freelance contributor writing a health and fitness column. It was great. From the first day when I went for my interview and met the quite elderly man named Fred who was the owner and publisher of the paper, to the first article I turned in, I felt comfortable there. Fred was a no-nonsense, outspoken, kind of guy. He had a gruff manner but if you looked very closely you could always detect a slight smile underneath his gruff exterior. I liked him immediately. The other big factor and attraction for choosing Wiseboro as previously mentioned, was the city's proximity to the scene of my crash. Someday I would be going there.

For my articles for Fred I had a byline under the name Annie Smith but a photo was never included. My articles eventually started to get picked up by bigger newspapers and franchises. That was pretty thrilling. I spent a lot of my time researching and trying out new recipes, researching food values, and listing the specific contents, and calories of everything I suggested in my articles. I joined a local gym where I met some new people. Over time I made some friends. One of those friends was Jennifer who ran the "Eat 'N' Run" cafe just down the street from my condo. Jennifer was single with no family close by. I was single with no family I wanted to have close by. As we had that in common it didn't take us long to find other things that made us become fast friends. It turned out Jennifer belonged to a card group. They met every Thursday evening with everyone taking a turn to host a card night. I had no idea if I knew how to play cards, but I was willing to give it a try. It was another thing, in a long list of things, I had no memory of.

I went along with Jennifer and joined the club. There was lots of laughter, good-hearted ribbing, beer, wine, and snacks. And as it turned out I was a pretty darn good card player. I won so many games that first night there were good-natured threats about banning me, or only allowing me to play half the games. At the following card nights I voluntarily stepped back from some rounds and sipped a nice glass of wine in a comfortable chair, while being steeped in the warmth of the friendly atmosphere.

Four months after I'd been in the card club a local Rec centre held a card tournament. Our group wanted to enter a team and talked me into being part of that team. I was a little worried about my anonymity being ruined and my new life being affected. Though, as it was just a little tournament in a local Rec centre I thought it would be fine. It wasn't fine. Some overzealous person decided the tournament should be part of the Social section in the "Recreation Events and Community" booklet that was always in coffee shops for free. In this instance a local had taken a picture of the tournament going on—and I was in the picture. The only saving grace to this possible disaster was that the picture was in black and white and my head was turned to the side.

When I decided to change my name and my life I considered changing my hair colour. I knew it was vain, as well as foolish, not too. However, for so long my sleek, thick, shoulder-length, red hair had been my crowning glory. It was entrenched as part of my identity. I couldn't do it. So I figured instead I would have to stay totally away from any cameras. I was in a city far enough away from the scene of my crash that it would be very unlikely any police officers or hospital staff from the crash would recognize me. And I was also far enough away from my previous big city home that I wasn't likely to be recognized by anyone. My family had always steered away from publicity because with great wealth comes the great fear of kidnapping. Very few people knew the exact extent of our wealth. That allowed our family to keep a low profile in society. Of course people knew we were rich but only a select few knew we were "over the top" rich. As no one came forward as having recognized me from the picture taken at the tournament I figured I had "dodged a bullet" there. I was so wrong as time would prove.

Chapter Five:
A Man With A Truck

My life continued along pretty well. I liked the people I worked with, and the people in the groups I joined. I even went out on a few dates, but nothing really clicked. That is, until one day I met a very attractive man.

I had a flat tire and had to call the dealer for my car about getting a tow. At the car dealership I was told they would call the tow truck company they used and send someone out to me immediately. The tow truck driver arrived, said hello, and started to hook my car up to the tow truck. Wow! This tow truck driver was so good looking. He had a great smile with perfect white teeth and when he smiled a dimple appeared in the corner of each cheek. Who couldn't love a very handsome man with dimples? With his blue eyes and crisp short black haircut he was good to look at. And to top it all off, this perfection was wrapped up in a tall, muscular body, wearing a red plaid work shirt and faded jeans. He was some hot looking tow truck driver. And he just seemed so nice.

He noticed the wheel rim of the flat tire was bent a bit and just slightly dented. I had noticed it and I had actually made an appointment with the dealer to have the rim replaced or repaired in the coming week. So, I guess there would already be an appointment booked at his shop for the repair. Funny thing, my vehicle would have come to his shop anyway. The tow truck driver then explained that if the valve stem was damaged that could have caused a slow leak in the tire which was an easy fix. I could have the car delivered or I could pick it up. As the shop was close by I said I would pick it up. I knew when the rim had been damaged. During a tremendous downpour a week or so before, on the rain slick road I had slid sideways with unbelievable speed, into a curb. The wheel rim had hit the cement curb edge with a real whack!

I guess I did have some snob in me from my upbringing because my first thought was too bad this guy is just a tow truck driver. Then I gave myself a talking to saying, "Stop it. The guy is doing an honest day's work and doing it well. Being a tow truck driver is a job that at times can be dangerous and requires professional skills to do the job right. Don't be such an entitled prig". I smiled at the tow truck driver and he smiled back.

The next day when I went to pick up my car there was the tow truck driver in the office looking like a million bucks. In an expensive suit and tie he looked like the epitome of class and success. Turns out he owned the automotive shop and tow truck business. He'd picked up my car because two of his mechanics were away on a training course and he was short handed. What a nice surprise! Really I wasn't too sure how much I would have had in common even with a great-looking tow truck driver. But I was pretty sure I could find something in common with the great-looking owner of a large, rich, thriving company. I guess it was my upbringing surfacing. I knew I should not equate a person's value with my thoughts about the kind of work they did. And I was really trying to not be that kind of person. I was working hard to make myself throw away my father's and sister's values, and to get rid of the biases of wealth that must have been ingrained in me since birth. But sometimes those ingrained biases just popped up unexpectedly.

When I walked into the office I was greeted with, "It's nice to see you again. I don't think I've ever seen you in this end of town before. By the way, my name is Jason. And I know your name is Annie from seeing it on the order for the tow."

I replied, "Nice to meet you Jason. I haven't lived in the city very long. I don't live too far from here. I actually walked over. The sun is so bright and the fall leaves are starting to turn. It's such a pretty day. A good day for a walk."

Jason nodded his agreement, then added, "I was just going to take a break and have a cup of coffee. Maybe you need one after your walk."

I laughed, "Well, it wasn't that far. But coffee does sound appealing. Thanks. That would be great."

"We have a little sunroom out on the back of the shop set up as a break room. It's a nice place to slow down for a few minutes and enjoy a good cup of coffee," continued Jason.

"Isn't it unusual to have a sunroom on the back of an automotive repair shop and towing business?" I asked.

"It is." Jason smiled, "One of my mechanics used to work as a landscaper. He decided it would be nice to have some place to sit for his break that had a view other than that of tires and machinery. He and his two brothers came one sunny Saturday and planted a few bigger trees and lots of shrubs. It looked so good I decided I should contribute. I got a bobcat in and removed the old cracked cement pad that had been here since my dad built the shop twenty years ago. Then I got rid of the old picnic table, wooden bench, and rickety old Adirondack chairs, which had been here forever. It looked so good I decided to keep going. I had a new cement pad poured and had a company come in to make a four season sun room with a fireplace. Then to finish it off, a decorator came in and made seating with washable covers so the men could come in from the shop on their breaks in their work clothes. The cleaners who come in daily change the seat covers. So it's safe to sit anywhere you like. Your jeans and jacket are safe. No shop grease to be afraid off."

"Having this sunroom" he continued, "has been very good for morale. Co-workers have developed deeper camaraderie and friendships. The area has been a great asset. And I would have to say I enjoy it as much as anyone. Now to get to the important stuff. I've got an insanely complicated coffee maker here. One of my guys is a coffee aficionado and requested this model. It has so many settings it may be possible to make jet fuel with it. I can make the basics with it; regular coffee, cappuccino, and Americana. That's about it. What's your preference?"

"I think a cappuccino would be perfect." I answered.

Jason smiled again, flashing those dimples, "Coming right up! And you're in luck today. There are still a few French pastries left. They generally are gone so fast it's as if they've vanished into thin air. The bakery around the corner brings in an assortment of buns, muffins, and pastries every morning. Come over and take your pick. The blueberry croissants seem to be the favourite. And surprisingly there are a few left today. Though really, everything is good. The little lady who owns the shop does a roaring business every morning. And rain or shine she always has our order here in time for morning coffee break."

Jason handed me the coffee in a heavy red mug and the pastry on a piece of paper towel.

At the first bite I said, "Oh man! This blueberry pastry is out of this world. And with my cup of cappuccino. I'm in heaven. So good." I said.

"I told you," he laughed. Then asked, "What do you do when you're not needing a tow truck?"

I replied, " I work at the Wiseboro Weekly as a freelance journalist. I write a health and fitness column. It's been a great job. I wanted to move to a smaller place to live. I previously worked for a large business firm, specializing in doing assessments of large properties.

The company was based in a much bigger city than Wiseboro. It was a high stress job. I wanted a change. So, here I am."

Jason said, "Wow, you really did do an about face. That's a pretty drastic change; not only in the job you're doing, but also in the place you're living. I commend you. It can be difficult to leave everything you know and make a fresh start."

Of course, Jason had no way of knowing I was not leaving everything I knew to move away. All I was leaving was a blank canvas with only my appearance and some very useful skills being taken with me to a new place. The saying is "You can't miss something you've never had" but in my case that didn't equate. I felt as though I was missing everything I had ever had, but with having no idea what that was, or how to retrieve it. Every day I mourned what I was missing; the life I had and knew, the good and the bad. But, everyday as I built a new life, I mourned the lack of knowledge of my old life a little bit less.

When I didn't comment right away I noticed Jason studying me. I quickly replied, "So far the experience couldn't be better. It's working out really well."

And with those words and a smile I said, " I had better be going. I have an article to get out in time for my byline today. So thanks again for the coffee and that pastry was delicious."

"It was my pleasure," said Jason. "I always try to stop for a break around 9:30. Then I generally let the guys have the room to themselves around 10:30. If you are out walking stop in for a coffee. I would be happy to pour you another one of my famous cappuccinos."

"That would be very nice. Thanks. I'll do that." I smiled.

Jason walked me out through the office and said good-bye.

"NICE", I thought to myself. I think I might have found something great. At first glance there was absolutely nothing I could see wrong with Jason. At first glance he seemed to be almost perfect. However, as there aren't many perfect people I should realistically lower my expectations somewhat. But still, he seemed to be a a pretty nice guy wrapped up in a a pretty nice package of handsomeness. Of course, if he is single, as I'm assuming he is—no wedding ring. Why? There is always a back story. Although I must say I'm looking forward to the journey of discovery of what that story might be. (I did eventually learn Jason had a long term relationship with his high school sweetheart for several years until they parted ways amicably.)

I showed up at the office that afternoon floating into work. I was thinking I could really like Jason. One day next week sunroom coffee would definitely be on my agenda.

Chapter Six:
Something Good

I started to stop in once a week for coffee with Jason. It was lovely to sit out back in the sun with our coffee and chat and laugh. The more I got to know Jason the more I liked him. I found out he had two sisters and two brothers. It sounded like his family got along very well. Which was a great deal different than my family experience. After the third week of me stopping by for coffee, Jason and I decided we should go out for dinner some night. Three days later as the sky was turning dark the buzzer for my condo rang. I buzzed Jason up. When I opened the door I was blown away by how good he looked. He was wearing a classic navy wool topcoat. With his charcoal dress pants and a navy cashmere v-neck sweater he was something to look at. I had thought he looked great as a tow truck driver and the scale just kept going up. He couldn't possibly have looked any better. And the best thing he was wearing was his smile. It made me feel warm all over.

We took Jason's car which was driven by his driver, a beefy man named Sam. I was thinking maybe Jason's driver, similar to my family's drivers, also had skills as a bodyguard. The driver dropped us at the Wellesby Hotel. It was a large, old, imposingly grand building that was built in the early 1900's to accommodate the wealthy, in the time of elegant train travel. The builders of the rail lines, those wealthy train magnates and entrepreneurs, dotted fancy hotels of this quality, in capital cities all across the country. And although some of the rail lines have been dismantled, re-directed, or totally abolished, these grand old buildings still stand as a testament to a different time when the railways were king and their owners lived like kings.

When Sam came around and opened our door we stepped out to be met by an older man with an upright military bearing. He was wearing a uniform of fine dark green wool with a row of polished gold buttons down the front of the jacket, and with gold buttons on his shoulder epaulets as well. With a "good evening" he opened the huge glass entry door for us. The door had a large ornate polished brass handle and a large polished brass door plate. With a smile he ushered us into the foyer.

The massive crystal chandelier at the top of the stairs, as we entered the building, was astonishing in its size and sparkle. As we continued on into the dining room the elegant, crystal lighting in the high, dark wood beamed ceiling, dropped subdued lighting into every corner of the large room. Everywhere you looked there were fabulous architectural finishes. The fine mahogany wood that edged the jewel coloured deep red, gold, and royal blue, velvet dining chairs was touched with a fine " gold leaf" design. There were inviting wing chairs also covered in velvet, in the same jewel tones, arranged around the massive fireplace at one end of the room. The thick "sink into" carpeting was in rich shades of deep red, gold, royal blue, cream, and jade. The colours were vibrant yet woven into the carpet in such a way as to be classically understated. The setting of the dining room was expensive, opulent, luxury. It was like entering a fairytale saturated with sophisticated class. This hotel, in this small capital city, certainly could give the huge hotels in much bigger cities a run for their money. And it could definitely give them some tips on timeless and total elegance in décor.

When we were seated in the dining room our waiter took our order beginning with a fine wine and ending with a fancy dessert. The dessert was made of strawberries and cream on a shortbread base, drizzled with a light rum sauce. As expected the meal was delicious. The service was of the highest quality. And the old world ambience surrounding us allowed us to share in a time when the good life was only for the very rich. It was magical. And being with Jason was the largest part of that magic.

When we arrived at my condo building Jason came up in the elevator with me. At the door he put his hands on my shoulders and gradually pulled me toward him. Then he kissed me. A kiss that started out softly and then turned into something much more. Then that kiss turned into another, and that kiss turned into another, and that turned into another. And the kisses were so good. Each one better than the one before. The kisses promised something wonderful. Suddenly, almost at the same time, Jason and I realized we were passionately making out in a very public hallway. We were clearly on view from the top floor atrium where people were relaxing among the greenery. And also on view from the large, open, secondary lobby that serviced the top floor. Not that we really cared or wanted to stop. But it did seem as if these kind of kisses were more for a private location. That private location should probably be the bedroom in my condo.

The problem was I wasn't quite sure enough of Jason to invite him totally into my life. If I did invite him into my life I would have to explain the circumstances and consequences of my memory loss; and my past, and what I didn't know about my past, and the life I had before meeting him. And how would that equate with me starting a new life, in a new place, with a new job? So far, I had managed to skate around giving definite answers to any questions that Jason had asked about my past life. But if I was to invite Jason into my bedroom I would have to do a lot of explaining. And then how would that go, if for some reason our love and romance didn't last? I would have a person out there who knew everything about me and my past. Which was exactly what I was trying to avoid. It was amazing how fast all those questions, answers, and thoughts flew across my mind as I was enjoying those absolutely marvellous kisses. It was hard to do but I made myself pull away from Jason. I could tell he was wondering why. He was obviously surprised. I mean the kisses were really something else and I was definitely fully participating.

I kept my arms around his neck as I stopped the last kiss saying, "Jason I do so like you, so, so, much. But, this is moving a little fast for me. My life was very different before I met you. And I'm working my way up to telling you about it. I'm not quite ready to do that yet. I'm sorry. I can't even express how much these kisses mean to me. They are wonderful. You are wonderful. I just need a little more time to sort things out. I hope you'll understand and be willing to wait. I think we might have something great".

Jason kept his hands on my waist. He looked at me with those gorgeous blue eyes. And then he softly said, " I'm not saying I'm not disappointed at how the evening is going to end. I'll admit I did have plans for something more than kisses on your doorstep. But I'm willing to wait until the time is right, looking forward to much more than kisses on the horizon."

His last comment filled me with a glow of anticipation. I was sure I would definitely like more than kisses with Jason. The thing was, I had to be absolutely sure before I shared my secrets with anyone. I had to have every little doubt totally, totally buried

Jason continued, "Good night for now. I'll look forward to seeing you tomorrow for coffee break."

With my arms still comfortably around his neck, and his hands still at my waist, I smiled and said, "I just had the best evening. It was lovely. I will also look forward to seeing you for coffee break tomorrow."

We had one long, last, "savouring" kind of kiss and I made myself remove my arms from his neck. With a last look I stepped inside and gently closed the door. Then just like in the movies I leaned with my back against the door hoping I could sense his presence until he was gone.

"Good grief!" I thought to myself, "I really must have it bad."

Chapter Seven:
Should I?

I did meet Jason for coffee break the next morning. And the glow was still there. In the next several weeks the amount of time I spent with Jason gradually increased. And eventually, on the night we became lovers I told Jason my story. As the evening closed in Jason and I were sitting close together on his cushy, buttery-soft, leather sofa. I told him about my barely functional family, my mother's death, how Edna had pretty much raised me at home, and about Gran. And then I told him I didn't remember any of it. Everything I knew about my past was from information and stories shared with me by other people; Gran, Janey, and Edna. I told him about my fear that the crash could have been an unsuccessful kidnapping attempt. And that frightening possibility, along with having no memory, and being tired of being labeled as that woman with amnesia, made me decide to separate myself from my unknown past and start fresh.

Jason sat in stunned silence for barely a second before he gathered me tightly in his arms.

He said, "My Annie, my Serafina. I'm so sorry for how your life changed so drastically. I'm glad you told me. I'm sure it wasn't easy to go through it all again. When you are ready, you and I will drive to the scene of the crash and see if it triggers any memories. Or, maybe you will find closure and pack the old life away forever. You're my Annie and I love you. We'll just keep building new memories together."

And as that statement settled around us we clasped hands, then walked to the bedroom to affirm the love we had been waiting to share. We were perfect together. Our lovemaking was sky rockets, violins and romantic dreams come true. As the days progressed we were doing all the silly things lovers do. We were sharing late night phone calls and sharing whispered secrets. It seemed we were continually smiling. We couldn't keep our hands off each other. I had found the one.

As Christmas approached we made plans to spend the holiday with Jason's family. We would arrive at his parent's home in the afternoon on Christmas Eve. The approaching event was slightly stressful for me as I had no experience celebrating holidays with a normal family. Edna had filled me in on the details of Christmas Day in my father's house. She said my father, my sister, and I, exchanged one gift each on Christmas morning in the library after breakfast. My gift from my father was the obligatory piece of jewellery. My sister's gift to me was a spa experience gift certificate. From me, my father received a box of Cuban cigars. Francine and I basically traded duplicate spa certificates. These gift choices never varied from year to year. We then separated going our separate ways until it was time for lunch. At twelve o'clock sharp my father, my sister, and I, gathered in the formal dining room for a traditional turkey dinner with all the traditional fixings of turkey, gravy, cranberries, and stuffing, finishing off with the traditional dessert of plum pudding with caramel sauce. The dinner didn't really work out very well for several reasons. As my sister Francine was a vegetarian she ate only salad and buns. My father was very careful about how much he ate in order to keep his trim figure. He hardly touched the meal at all. And I took only some of the basic items without any of the gravy or heavy pudding. Christmas dinner was considered what you should do for your Christmas experience. Christmas dinner was a tradition. And even though no one enjoyed it the Douglas traditions had to be maintained.

Edna said after lunch was over I would slip down to the kitchen to spend time with her. That's where the real Christmas Day was. Then as we did when my mother was with us, we would experience some of her wonderful Christmas baking of assorted decorated cookies and chocolate covered treats. Every year Edna gave me a new journal as she knew, even at a young age, writing was something I enjoyed. Along with the journals Edna's present always included something handmade, a soft throw, a crocheted scarf, or a knit sweater. I had found some of those items in my bedroom. It was lovely to now know where they had come from. Apparently my gift to Edna ever since I was a small child was a handwritten poem or a short story. And with a smile on her face as she told me that she had saved every one, Edna then handed me a beautiful little craft box covered with lace and embroidered pansies. It was filled with my written gifts to her. She thought maybe if I looked through them something might jog my memory. No luck.

Edna told me that as I grew older and had access to my own bank account, I started to buy her small delicate pieces of jewellery. Her face lit up as she described some of the beautiful pieces I had given her. She said when I came back from Christmas at Jason's we would sit in her snug little sitting room and go through the pieces together. Something lovely to look forward too.

This year things would be different for my family, me and Edna. As I would be away with Jason on Christmas Day I left the wrapped gifts for my father and sister in the library. I wouldn't miss seeing them. Then I went to the kitchen early on Christmas Eve morning so Edna and I could still spend time together.

As Edna spent Christmas afternoon and evening with her sister's family she always left a cold supper in the fridge for the Christmas

Day meal for my father and sister. It just needed to be heated up. Fat chance of that happening! It was expected. But it was a wasted endeavour as my father always spent Christmas evening at his Club and now that Francine was an adult, she went bar hopping with her group, or to some barely respectable party. I always went to see Janey and her family and Gran. This year I would see them after Christmas. I would not be missed by my father or sister.

Jason's story was much different than mine in so many ways. When Jason's father retired Jason's mom and dad moved to a large acreage on the outskirts of the city. I had been there with Jason once for supper but I didn't know all the family members. I had never met his two sisters and two brothers. Jason had told me a little bit about each of them, saying his sisters and brothers were very career driven and very successful in their chosen fields. He didn't have any nieces and nephews. And Jason said although it was seldom mentioned, his parents were quietly and eternally hopeful that one day they would have grandchildren.

On one hand I was looking forward to a real family Christmas. On the other hand it was a nerve wracking idea to be spending time in such close quarters with people I didn't know. I wasn't familiar with the concept of having family occasions that were happy and fun-filled.

I spent a lot of time looking through my wardrobe and picking out things that would be suitable for a family gathering at an acreage. I finally settled on casual slacks and a soft pale pink sweater for Christmas Eve. In my opinion you can never go wrong with pink! I had an emerald green slim fitting sheath dress that would be perfect for Christmas supper. So I was set.

Chapter Eight:
Meet the family

Jason and I arrived at his family home on the afternoon of Christmas Eve. Even through the uncomfortable first hellos and hugs I could feel the warmth of my welcome. This was a family that supported each other. I could feel that as I was Jason's choice, I would be their choice also. There was a bit of a complication in that all Jason's brothers and sisters had names that started with "J". Jarrod was the oldest, Julie was next, then Jason, Jordan, and Janine. And what a good-looking group they were. They all had the striking "black Irish" good looks with midnight black hair, sky blue eyes, and fair complexions. I'd never thought of Jason as having Irish heritage, although the name of the towing company, "Kelly Automotive and Towing" should have been a hint! Mrs. Kelly was the outlier in the family, with a beautiful English rose complexion, light blue eyes and blonde hair. Obviously the heritage of Mr. Kelly had been the dominant gene in that match-up. They were such a welcoming, jovial group. It was wonderful to be included, although a little over-whelming. I had come from a household with an austere father and a whiny, dissatisfied sister. There was no laughter or friendly teasing in my home. Here there was a lot of good- hearted joking and witty conversation. As we settled in the large living room in front of the fireplace the cross-talking between the comfy sofas was quite something. I was totally out of my element but it was fascinating. Such an eclectic group but with such obviously strong ties of affection.

Jarrod was an optometrist, Julie had a medical clinic she owned and operated. Jordan was a criminal lawyer and Janine owned several expensive, elite, clothing boutiques under the name "Janine's". They were all successful in their own right. As we were called into supper it didn't take long to see who ran the show at family gatherings. It was very obviously the "English Rose" who directed life in the family. In a quietly efficient manner she directed, organized, and settled the family to the business of enjoying an absolutely lovely meal. The table setting was gorgeous, all upper class English elegance showing Mrs. Kelly's upper class English roots. I was sure there must be a story there about Irish meets English. I would ask Jason later how his mom and dad had met.

The linens on the table were snowy white with fine lace edgings. The crystal was so fine and delicate you could hear it ring at the slightest touch. The white china, as well as the crystal wine glasses, and water goblets, were edged with an intricate hand painted design of holly and ivy. The meal was a traditional turkey dinner with all the trimmings. There was one deviation. Instead of traditional plum pudding cranberry cheese cake was served. Ummm. And that was fine with me! Apparently the change was made years ago. It seemed the children had never liked plum pudding. And after many Christmases with most of the plum pudding left uneaten on their plates Mrs. Kelly felt there needed to be a change. So, a family consensus was taken and the dessert was changed. The conversation throughout the meal was entertaining and the food was delicious. In her previous life, before her marriage, Mrs. Kelly had been an apprentice to a highly regarded chef in a very exclusive restaurant. In this family talent was around every corner it seemed !

When the meal drew to a close everyone helped clear the table. Everything was taken into the kitchen. The Kellys' live-in housekeeper would finish the clean-up in the morning before she went across town to spend Christmas Day with her family. As everyone settled themselves comfortably back in the living room Jarrod and Janine stood up. With their arms around each other's waists and "the cat that swallowed the canary" smiles on their faces, Jarrod spoke first.

He said, " Janine and I each have an announcement to make, which I'm sure will make everyone extremely happy".

He continued, "My announcement is that my beautiful wife Cassandra and I are expecting a baby in August". The gasps of surprise and the smiles of joy were immediate. Before anyone could speak Janine joined in quickly saying, " And Tom and I are also having a baby in August as well. So, there will be two new little people here next Christmas who will be enlarging the Kelly clan!"

Following that statement I happened to look over at the elegant Mrs. Kelly sitting on the corner sofa. She was smiling at Mr. Kelly sitting in the wing chair across from her. As I watched I saw her silently mouth the words "finally grandchildren" and where her hand was resting on the sofa cushion I saw her make an inelegant, forceful, "thumbs up" gesture. Mr. Kelly returned her smile and nodded his head in agreement with both her silent words and her gesture.

After this exciting news was shared the room exploded with questions, congratulations, hugs, and kisses. This hubbub was immediately followed by phone calls to Jarrod and Janine's spouses with everyone having a chance to extend their congratulations. Later I asked Jason why Jarrod and Janine were here alone. Apparently Jarrod's wife Cassandra was in Europe at a convention for a charitable organization she was involved with. She wouldn't be home until after New Year's Day. Janine's husband was also away. He was working with a humanitarian organization in Nigeria and wouldn't get home until the middle of January. The two couples had wanted to share their good news when the family was together.

This whole visit was a bit of a reversal for me. In my home we had our traditional turkey dinner on Christmas Day. But, because some of the family had to travel home on Christmas Day, in the Kelly family, Christmas Eve became the big event day with the formal supper. After the big announcements and a lot of baby talk, the next several hours were filled with lively conversation sprinkled with bursts of laughter against a background of soft Christmas music. I wasn't required to say much, yet I felt totally included. I was entertained as a watcher of the family dynamics. Jarrod definitely still had the role of the wise older brother. Julie was like his second in command. Jason was the more relaxed, "easy to get along with anyone" brother. Jordan was definitely his own man with a little different take on every topic discussed. And Janine still had a bit of that "I'm the baby", "I'm special", kind of attitude. But they all seemed to be good with that. As a matter of fact they all seemed to be totally accepting of each other. And it was obvious they enjoyed each other's quirks and personalities. I found that to be really something. They were such a likeable lot. I was impressed.

As the evening wound down everyone said goodnight and wandered off to their respective rooms. Jason and I said our good nights and headed off to our room. A happy, contented, feeling wrapped around us. And as we snuggled under the "soft as air" thick down coverlet we pledged our love with words and actions. We fell asleep nose to nose with arms clasped around each other.

We awoke to jingling bells. The traditional Kelly call to Christmas breakfast. And what a breakfast it was! The table was so laden it should have sagged in the middle. Every item was top-chef worthy delicious. Again, after having tasted some of everything breakfast had to offer, the table was cleared and everything was taken to the kitchen to be dealt with later. Then the traditional Christmas music playing softly in the background spun the perfect ambience for opening presents. Everyone found a seat and Mr. Kelly played Santa passing out the gifts from under the tree. Eventually the Oohs!, Ahhs!, exclamations of incredulity, cries of joy, and spurts of laughter, gave way to a quieter tone as everyone knew it would soon be time to leave. There was a final round of coffee and treats, then everyone started to gather up their gifts, clean up the wrapping paper, and head upstairs to get their packed suitcases.

It had been a wonderful experience, being included as part of a loving family. It was sad to see it end but all the way home I carried that new found wealth of family with me. And I had Jason. So life was good.

Chapter Nine:
The Unexpected Happens

Life returned to normal. Jason and I were becoming more in love with each passing day. We were trying to make a decision on which condo we should move into, his or mine, or buy new. Both of our condos were located in excellent locations, which made the decision a little more difficult. Finally we decided if we could find a new place with "location, location, location" as the realtors say, we would definitely buy something new to start our life together. That decision was put aside when Jason had to go on a business trip. Jason's family not only owned an automotive repair shop and towing business. It came to light the Kelly family had business interests in Saudi Arabia having to do with oil. It was a start-up company run by Anwar, Jason's friend from university. Jason was the point man and contact for the joint venture. Most of the business was done through long distance measures, but occasionally Anwar would come to Wiseboro or every couple of years Jason would fly to Saudi Arabia. I was thinking these Kellys must be really, really rich. Probably richer than my family if they had an oil company. When I asked Jason about owning an oil company he said it definitely wasn't a big deal. It was just an investment in a very small company. The trip Jason was taking this time was because Anwar was getting married. It was as much to attend his friend's wedding as to see how the business was progressing. Jason and his university buddy were very close. The company was doing well, though on a much smaller scale than is usually thought of for Saudi companies.

Jason wanted me to come with him. He thought we could make it a holiday and he could show me the wonders of Saudi Arabia. He was disappointed when I didn't want to go. I just couldn't. I was barely starting to find my feet as a person missing memories of her entire life. The thought of a trip thousands of miles away to a foreign land was just too unsettling and too intimidating. I was just finding my way in a new life with some feeling of security. I said maybe I would be ready to go next time. Jason was disappointed. But Jason was a caring man with an empathetic nature. So, he said he understood, and added that there would be lots of other opportunities to visit such an interesting country together. We could go another time if I felt I wanted to give it a try. The night before Jason left our loving was, if possible, filled with more meaning and love than ever before, hoping to stave off thoughts of being apart. I took him to the airport and watched him disappear into the atmosphere.

I mean he really did disappear. The cameras inside the airport showed Jason walking through the airport heading toward the large front door exit. After that there was nothing. In a case of very bad luck or perhaps sinister behaviour, the cameras showing the exterior of the building were off for a few minutes while a glitch in the security system was being fixed. Anwar had been held up in traffic and when he arrived to pick up Jason outside the front exit Jason was nowhere to be seen. Anwar left his driver with the car and went inside to find Jason. When he had no luck he contacted airport security who put out a message asking Jason to report to the security desk. Jason did not appear. Because kidnapping is a very real threat in Saudi Arabia Anwar was starting to panic. Jason did not have any security with him as Anwar's family would supply him with their security while he was in Saudi Arabia. That seemed to have been a big mistake.

Anwar contacted his father so his father could contact the police. When Anwar spoke to his father he was given some very startling, terrifying news. Apparently a Saudi mafia group had grabbed Jason and had then contacted Anwar's father demanding a ransom for Jason's return. How they knew about Jason and the details of his trip, such as his arrival time was unknown. But many mafia groups have networks reaching into every sector of society, at home and abroad. And now a huge problem loomed. It turned out Anwar's family was very much less wealthy than they appeared to be. Anwar's family was struggling to keep up their appearance of wealth to hold on to their place in Saudi society. His family had put most of their financial resources into the small oil company. That had almost cleaned them out. The returns they had expected from the company were much smaller than expected, and also much slower in appearing.

Speed was of the essence so Anwar's father urgently contacted Jason's father. Jason's father had the amount for the ransom and immediately agreed to provide it. The deal was set for the money transfer of the ransom. The deadline of forty-eight hours for the deal to transfer the money came and went, and was met with total silence from the mafia group. It made no sense. The mafia was getting the money. But they were never heard from again. And Jason stayed disappeared! The Saudi government was really no help at all. Jason's father was stonewalled at every turn. The government always pleading ignorance and having no information to give. The Saudis just wanted the incident to go away. They didn't want it known that anyone coming to do business in Saudi Arabia might disappear. They wanted their global reputation protected.

Back home both the Kelly family and I were flooded with despair. Time passed, then more time passed, then more time passed and still no news of Jason, his whereabouts, or his possible death. It was so mind numbing to think I'd never see Jason again. And maybe never know what had happened to him. All hope of Jason being alive was fading a little more with every passing occasion; birthdays, Christmas, the anniversary of the day we met, and the anniversary of the day he disappeared. After Jason disappeared it took months for me to adjust to being without him. Every time I went by Kelly's Automotive and Towing I'd burst into tears. That problem helped me with my decision to leave the neighbourhood. I got a new condo on the other side of the city. Far away from the lovely coffee breaks in the shop sunroom. The halcyon days of smiles and sunshine were gone. In reality life does go on and some way has to be found to soften the heartache. To find something solid to hold onto again in my life, I started to focus on trying to get even a tiny piece of my memory back. And that caused me to make several trips to the site of my car crash.

As the time of Jason's disappearance kept lengthening I was once again at the crash site. Although it seemed impossible, the tire tracks from my car were still slightly visible, as were the tire tracks of the much heavier vehicle that had rammed my car. That was quite something. I was sure time and weather would have removed those marks entirely. As I stood by the crime scene nothing came to me. Nothing clicked. I stood there willing myself to remember something. Finally, I had to admit defeat. My memory was gone and never coming back. It was time to quit coming here. And as I was thinking those thoughts I noticed a large black truck that was partially hidden by the distant tree line, turning onto the narrow road where I was parked. As I was noticing the black truck coming toward me at a very fast rate of speed suddenly I felt very exposed. I got into my car, locked the doors, rolled up the window, and just as I was putting the car into drive the huge black truck that seemed to be heading straight for me, sped on past spraying gravel from the edge of the road as it passed by. In the distance I could see another vehicle coming toward me.

For some reason that black truck had triggered terror in my heart. As I took a deep breath and tried to slow it's beating, I heard a rumbling sound that seemed vaguely familiar. And as I was thinking that thought a very old looking, light blue, half ton truck came rumbling down the road toward me. I had a slight tingling feeling of déjà vu. For some reason the sound seemed familiar. And also the feeling of being out alone on an isolated road, feeling the urge to get back into my vehicle and turn back to the town, was also familiar. I did a u-turn, and started slowly moving back down the gravel road to the town. As the old half ton slowed to a stop beside me the driver motioned for me to roll down the window. I rolled my window down a crack as the driver of the half ton leaned over to call to me.

He said, "Hello, I'm so glad to see you. You don't know me, but I know you. (I guess another person missing from my memory bank) My name is Nate Kendall. I was the person who found you at the edge of the road after your car was crashed. I was working under-cover for the DEA at the time and could not reveal my name or location. That's why I had to drop you off at the hospital anonymously. If you feel you want to know the details of that night, as many as I know, please call me. I can use my real name now safely. I'm listed in the phone directory. I would be happy to meet you for coffee and a talk".

I was shocked as I listened to this stranger.

I replied after my jaw quit dropping, "That would be great. Thank-you. I will do that."

The man tapped the brim of his cap, smiled, and drove away. I didn't move a muscle for a full ten minutes. This was unbelievable. Maybe a chance to find out some new information about my life was on the horizon. When I got home I did look up Nate Kendall's phone number. I suddenly couldn't wait to call. I dialled and the smooth baritone voice of the driver of the half ton answered. We made a date to meet the next day at the "Drop In" cafe on Centre street in the city at 10 a.m.

I was there early sitting in a booth with red leatherette seats in a back corner of the café. The tall, lanky Nate Kendall was right on time. He smiled and removed his cap as he sat down. Such an old fashioned courteous gesture. The man was actually gorgeous; with dark blonde hair, hazel eyes, and a great smile. As he sat and leaned his forearms on the table I could see under that lanky build was a buff body of sinew and strength. This man was the whole package. I couldn't believe I was thinking such thoughts. Wasn't one heartbreak enough? My true love was lost to me and here I am ogling a strange man. It would be disloyal to Jason to feel an attraction to someone I had just met! Removing thoughts of attraction from my mind I returned Nate's greeting of "hello", and turned my attention to the important business at hand.

Nate started by saying, " I did know who you were after reading the newspapers. But I was deep undercover, hiding out until some "over the top" bad people were caught and convicted. I had infiltrated a gang of the worst of the worst. Unfortunately my cover was blown. And I was in isolation in the forest, seldom leaving my hideaway. I happened to be driving my old blue work truck, taking a chance to stock up on some supplies, the day I found you. I could get supplies at a tiny grocery store on the outskirts of town run by a friend. Later, when the people I was hiding from were caught you had disappeared. There was no information on where Serafina Douglas had gone".

"I did disappear," I said. "I woke up with no memory of my life before the crash. I was tired of being labelled as "the woman who had amnesia". I wanted to start fresh. I changed my name, got a new job, and moved to a new city."

" I did read that you suffered from amnesia after your accident. I can't even imagine how difficult that would be. It was probably a smart idea to find a new place to live and to start over." Nate continued. "I'm also starting over. I made a big change too. I left my secure career with the DEA to become an entrepreneur. Which was in fact, kind of frightening. Now there is actually a road to where I live. The forest has been partially cleared. And the old cabin where I looked after you, before taking you to the hospital, is now a large lodge that is part of a small resort. The resort is gaining a reputation as a popular tourist destination. The small resort I've developed has become a nature adventure destination. It is also popular as a destination for corporate conventions, group getaways, and nature retreats."

Nate added, "After living in the forest for a year I found I really liked it. Life in the forest is very isolated, but also very peaceful. The foliage is beautiful. The wildlife is so enjoyable to watch and study. I have found the forest to be a very peaceful, contemplative place to live. Which was quite a shock as I was always very much a city boy. That was one of the reasons it was so easy for me to infiltrate into a big city criminal gang. It was also how my cover was blown, because someone from the city recognized me.

At first I found the isolation of the deep forest very disheartening. As time passed I grew to love it. And now with my tourism business I have the best of both worlds. I can socialize and be with people, which is something I always enjoy. That was something I really missed when I was in hiding. Or I can shut out the world for a time to enjoy the peace and beauty of life beside a clear lake in my green palace. I do still have a small place in the city. It's hard to totally take the city out of the boy."

"When I heard your truck rumbling down the road it seemed as if I remembered the sound. It was almost a memory." I said softly.

"But as quickly as the edge of a memory flitted past I felt feelings of terror and pain." I added.

Nate nodded saying, "I was driving that rumbling truck the day I found you. So, maybe that actually is a partial memory. That afternoon I saw something bright pink at the edge of the road. It turned out to be your arm in a bright pink jacket. It's lucky your arm was visible or you could have been lying there for hours. That would not have been good. You were bleeding quite heavily from a cut on the back of your head."

"Yes, the doctors said that someone with medical knowledge had put pressure on the wound to stop the blood flow, likely saving my life. So I owe you a deep debt of gratitude. Thank you." I said.

Nate replied, "I was glad I was there to help. I laid you in the box of the truck and took you to my cabin until it was dark. Then I could take you to the hospital. Of course, I was very curious to find out who you were and what had caused the crash. The details of who you were and the crash were very sketchy on the news. They did give out your name. And there was one article where someone gave out the information that there was temporary memory loss for you as a result of the crash. That's sensitive, private information, which I'm sure shouldn't have been released. I would guess someone was reprimanded over that."

"Yes, it was pretty bad," I agreed. "Having my memory loss publicly known made my life uncomfortable. I was the oddity in the office, and pretty much everywhere I went, particularly for the first few months after the accident. And even as time passed it always seemed there was a slight, ongoing undercurrent, about my condition. So I moved on. I moved far away from the big city to Wiseboro. One of the crazy reasons I chose it was because it was close to the crash site. I thought maybe if I could visit the crash site a few times I would remember something. Unfortunately I haven't remembered anything. As you drove up I had just decided to give it up. Make that my last visit there."

Nate thoughtfully said, " You have to do what your heart tells you. Sometimes that is the best way to make decisions that change our lives."

I agreed, "I can't keep going around and around in circles in my mind hoping things will change. Yesterday at the site I decided I was done with trying to retrieve my old life and I was fully going to embrace the new life I have. Today is a new start."

"I'm glad to hear that," said Nate "Because that means hopefully, I am part of your new start. We've already got a history together like few others have. I'd be very interested to get to know Annie Smith."

I smiled and said, "I think that could be arranged. I'd like to get to know the person who saved my life."

Returning my smile Nate said, "I think we should celebrate that idea by adding a big, gooey cinnamon bun to our coffee. And I'm just the guy to get us one."

As Nate walked away I couldn't help but admire his lanky stride in a good-looking, good-fitting, pair of faded jeans.

Chapter Ten:
Mystery Solved

Not long after I met Nate a part of my life that had come unravelled was explained.

Things were going so well with Nate. Strangely, I still, often had the feeling someone was watching me. I just shook it off as I never saw anything out of the ordinary. I did however take extra care noticing the people around me, and my surroundings, always remembering the possibility my crash could have been a kidnapping attempt.

One morning when I was leaving early for work, as I parked my car in the empty office lot, my internal warning system made me feel strongly that this time I actually was being watched. I casually made my way to a top floor office and unobtrusively looked out to study the street. There was a large, heavy black truck partially hidden at the edge of an office building, beside an empty lot, one block down. Suddenly my heart started beating so fast as I stood hidden at the corner of that window and watched the truck. Nothing happened. No one moved near, in, or out of, the truck. It could be that I was overreacting. But too many black truck coincidences seemed to be happening.

I called Nate. I had told him that with my crash there had always been the possibility (though pooh- poohed by the local police) that my crash could have been a kidnapping gone wrong. Nate took my woman's intuition about being watched to heart. He contacted two of his old DEA buddies, Devon and Matt, to take on surveillance of me as a sideline. I paid them and they watched over me. Nate wanted to pay out of his pocket, as they were his friends, but it was my problem. And I was certainly able to pay. It was about time some of the Douglas riches sitting in my bank account were put to something useful.

Devon and Matt shadowed me for two weeks and on the last Friday of the second week they got a good look at the driver of the truck. He was known to police. He was the leader of a small band of hoodlums, most of whom had been caught in various criminal activities in the past and spent time in jail. This group was known to police. They were usually looking for the easy mark, the quick score. If they were involved in a kidnapping attempt of me, they were certainly shooting higher than their usual efforts. It wasn't surprising they had screwed it up. They had smashed a valuable vehicle and nearly ended up killing their target.

Because of the limited skills of this group, how could they have hoped to pull off kidnapping me? I had great non-intrusive security with me at all times. With further investigation Matt and Devon found the source of the group's information on my activities. What was uncovered was that two of the group had infiltrated my father's household as two new gardeners. And over several months they had been watching my schedule. The idea was that I would eventually go somewhere on my own. The group was in no hurry. The big payday would make it worth their while to wait. This group had lots of smaller on-going scams to keep the organization going while they were waiting for an opening to grab me.

Ordinarily they could have waited forever and never gotten close to me on my own. It was just bad karma for me, and good luck for them, that I did something very unusual. And something most would consider stupid (as I did now) getting in a car and driving myself. If I hadn't carelessly grabbed that little piece of freedom, this criminal group would never have caught me alone.

Now that the premise had changed from the thinking that my accident was an attempted carjacking to an attempted kidnapping, the crash was looked at from a different angle. Probably the expectation of the hopeful abductors had been that I would stop when the threatening black truck tried to force me to the side of the road. That backfired for them because I tried to outrun them and it backfired for me because I almost died.

After the accident I had basically dropped out of sight. How did this group of criminals find me? Pure luck. It seems that picture I was a little worried about taken at the Rec card tournament was something I definitely should have been worried about. When the criminals were interviewed by the police it came out that one of the men involved in the kidnapping attempt picked up a copy of the "Recreation Events and Community" free booklet off a gas station counter when passing through Wiseboro. While flipping through the booklet as he had his lunch in the gas station café, he recognized my picture at the card tournament. He told his boss and the kidnapping was back on. Now that Devon and Matt had identified the group, and in particular the driver of the truck, all that was required was to follow the truck as it followed me. A week later the driver of the truck surreptitiously followed me across the parking lot at work. As he came near to me Matt and Devon grabbed him. It didn't take much for the police to get a confession from the driver of the truck, as the punishment would be very severe for an attempted kidnapping. The police sweetened the pot for the driver with a lesser sentence, if he confessed and gave up his co-conspirators. Which he did in the blink of an eye.

An exploding revelation occurred when I saw a picture of the criminal who had been driving the big black truck. I remembered him!! I remembered him!! I remembered him looking down at me as I lay bleeding in the weeds at the edge of the road. I couldn't believe it! I remembered him!

And that was the start. Memories of the crash started to resurface. But also bits and pieces of my life before the crash started to return. By the time the criminals had been tried and sentenced I had crystal clear memories of my life before the crash! What a new world view. I was whole again. Every day I remembered more. It was like opening the trove of a treasure chest of wonder. I would never again take having memories for granted. It was lovely to have Nate by my side as I rediscovered my previous life. He really was the hero of my life. As the wonder of my memory became more normal to me, the relationship of Nate and I moved on.

Chapter Eleven:
Life Goes On

Occasionally, when I considered the two men in my life to whom I had whole heartedly given my heart, in some ways they were very different. Yet, in every way that really counted they were very much the same.

Jason and Nate were completely different in looks and style. Jason always looked very cosmopolitan, always smartly dressed, always classy. He looked like a high roller executive on time away from the office even in old jeans and a ratty t-shirt. He often worked in the shop with the guys if the car they were working on interested him. Covered in grease he still looked great. Nate always looked more outdoorsy, as if he had just come in from a walk in the fresh air. Which he probably had. He also was a car guy. And I would have to say grease looked good on his lanky frame also.

They were both entrepreneurs. Jason grew up in the automotive business but the continued success of the business rested squarely on his shoulders. Nate went from paid employment as a DEA officer to strike out on his own and build a successful business with no help from anyone.

.

They both had a great sense of humour. Nate had a quiet smile which sometimes broke out into a gutsy laugh making everyone else laugh along with him. I seldom heard Jason laugh, but I very often saw him smile. Jason wasn't a real "laugh out loud" kind of guy. Jason was more likely to get a twinkle in his eye, smile with those dimples, and come out with a comment that would make the person he was talking to "crack up" with laughter. You couldn't help but enjoy the joke along with him.

Someone once told me a man with a sense of humour is golden. I guess I found gold twice.

Jason and Nate differed distinctly in some of their interests and activities. Nate was into hiking, biking, and kayaking, anything outdoors. Nate liked a casual lifestyle where jeans were suitable for every occasion.

Jason liked to work out at the gym and was a "scratch" golfer. Which I learned means an elite golfer. He was also a swimmer as I was. We had both grown up with pools at home. I excelled at swimming and became a high profile swimmer at college. Both our condos had pools. So, when we moved in together swimming had been something we did every day. It didn't matter where we were, or where we were visiting, if there was a pool Jason was in it.

Jason and Nate's backgrounds were totally different. Nate grew up in a middle income family. He had to make his way to success without a hand up from anybody. His family was very close, but very small.

Jason took over a well-established business and increased its success. He came from a large family. Something Jason and I had in common was that we were both children of wealth. And we enjoyed the trappings of wealth; the luxuries of great housing, great wardrobes, and expensive dinners out. We would travel to an exotic destination on a whim. Though Jason and Nate were different in many ways, their greatest similarity was their empathy for others, their innate kindness, and their love for me. In those things Jason and Nate were two sides of the same coin.

Not unexpectedly Nate's and my relationship started slowly and in a similar manner to Jason's and mine. We became coffee friends, then lunch friends. Then before we became romantic friends I told Nate everything I had been told about my life before the crash. And also how absolutely nothing had come back to me. Eventually I introduced Nate to Janey and Gran and told him about Jason and Jason's disappearance. Janey and Gran were so pleased I had found a great guy like Nate. Nate was so easy-going and easy- to-like, leading to moving forward to being easy- to-love. It took me a while to admit my true feelings to myself and then to Nate. (I still carried that underlying feeling of guilt about being happy with Nate. It was like I was being disloyal to Jason. But Jason was gone.) I never thought I could love anyone like I loved Jason, but Nate was a wonderful guy and he proved me wrong. When we finally did totally commit to each other it was at his resort in his king size bed with a cozy fire dancing in the huge fireplace. We were in love. And our loving was splendid! In the afterglow of coming together we whispered our devotion and plans for our future. It was a beautiful night. One to be remembered forever.

After the kidnapping attempt was blocked and my memory returned, the relationship of Nate and I was even better, if that was possible. Because once again I was my whole self. There were no empty spaces in the picture parade of my life.

Our life progressed happily. And as I only needed to be in the office in person about two days a week I started to stay with Nate at his resort most nights and every weekend. It was an enchanting place, a true gem in the forest. As soon as work was over I was on my way to Nate's. That summer we were together as much as possible. We went kayaking and swimming in the cold, clear, lake at his resort. And we did a lot of great hiking and exploring. On one of our hikes we found some hidden caves and some great fossils. On another trip we discovered a small hidden waterfall falling into a tiny, clear, deep pool. In the evenings we enjoyed lovely dinners outside on his private deck under a brilliant moon with twinkling fairy lights sprinkled amongst the trees. When Fall settled in we spent our time bike riding, swimming in the resort's huge indoor pool, and having late night bonfires under a starry sky. On the coldest nights we bundled up under a big quilt for added warmth to sit outside by the fire. As winter approached we still hiked and enjoyed evening bonfires, but most evenings we could be found sitting side by side on a big, comfy, sofa, in front of the fire reading books. Now that was something totally different from Jason.

Jason seldom sat still to read. And if he did read, it was more likely to be articles in the three or four magazines he subscribed to. He loved to be up on the top news stories and the latest developments in vehicle advancements; new motors, new chassis, whatever was new and exciting in the vehicle industry. And although it didn't seem to fit exactly with his other interests he was very interested in wildlife and wild life preservation. His choice would not be sitting around a bonfire each evening. Although occasionally he might enjoy it. He wasn't above enjoying a bonfire. But rather Jason's preference would be to go out for an exceptional meal at an exceptional restaurant. Or he would cook a gourmet meal for me at home. Jason, like me, was interested in healthy eating and the best ways to enjoy it. He was a man of many talents. And perhaps the best talent of all was that because he loved all types of music, he also liked to dance. What a gift that was. A man who liked to dance. Jason said a favourite aunt had taught him some years before she passed away. When he was little his aunt put his small feet on her bigger feet and danced him around the room. I think I would have liked that aunt.

There was one thing that was quite a difference between Jason and Nate. Jason never played cards. It was not an activity he had ever been involved in. When he was growing up his family didn't play cards. And when he was older he had been too busy with other things. Also, he didn't have any friends who were card players. It was a skill he didn't have and didn't miss. Gran told me that she taught me to play. I was brought up playing cards with Gran and her card group.

Nate was a card player. Although his family were not card players, he had learned later in life during stake-outs in his DEA service. And he was good. I introduced him to my card group. They embraced him with open arms, always looking for new blood to grow the club. He thought it was a real laugh that I recused myself from one-half to two-thirds of the games so other members would have a chance to win. After a few weeks of participation when he was comfortable with the group, Nate joined in the good- natured teasing to me about me being the card whisperer or the Stephen Hawking of card playing. He always joked to me that he didn't mind being the side-kick to the star. Through all the kidding I knew he was proud of my exceptional skill.

As Christmas approached again things were very different in my life. Now I had Nate. Jason was still missing. And although it was never spoken aloud I'm sure everyone felt Jason was gone forever. Jason's family did keep in touch with me. As there was no news and Jason was our only tie, the length of time between our conversations continued to stretch. No one had given up, but our hope had turned to "almost" acceptance that we would never see Jason again.

I made myself put Jason in a comfy, safe corner of my heart to be forever cherished. Then I welcomed Nate into the rest of my heart wholeheartedly. That was the only way life could go on without Jason. And Nate was a "top of the line" guy. He had stolen my heart in a totally different way than Jason, but stolen it he had. And I was in love with him.

As the days to Christmas moved closer both Nate and I were getting excited to see his family. Nate's parents would be away on a cruise they had won on a local lottery ticket. That meant they would miss Christmas but they would be home a few days before

New Year's in time to celebrate with the family. Nate had a sister named Sally who was a nurse, a brother-in-law named Alex, who was an electrical engineer, and a delightful five year old niece named Mathilda. I got to know the family through joining in on some of the family phone calls with Nate. And also through the pictures and letters they exchanged. Every letter had a picture from Mathilda for Uncle Nate and Aunt Annie. I felt quite honoured. The little family was coming to stay for a week at Nate's resort. We had all kinds of activities planned for Mathilda; bonfires, wiener roasts, sledding, skating on the lake. But as she was coming from the Yukon where she had done all those things, we decided to provide lots of indoor activities, with different crafts, lots of time in the indoor pool and hot tub, and visits to some fancy restaurants, movie theatres and the bowling alley. Things all four adults could enjoy as well.

Of course, my Christmas would involve spending time with Gran, Edna, and Janey and her family. Janey's daughter Rosie was the same age as Mathilda which should work out well, as I intended to introduce Nate's family to these special people in my life. As my father and sister had never tried to contact me in my new life I wouldn't be bothering with them. Everything was arranged ands set. It seemed like a great holiday was planned; seeing family and friends, enjoying everything a happy Christmas has to offer.

Chapter Twelve:
My World Was Rocked

It was Christmas morning and I kissed Nate then slipped away before his family was up and about. I wanted to see Edna before she left for her sister's. And what was so great was that now I remembered that was what I had always done. I remembered! As I absolutely did not want to see my father or the wicked sister Francine I slipped into the house through the lower level back door into the kitchen. As usual Edna was waiting with a big hug and a tray of special Christmas baking, the same as every Christmas morning throughout my life. And now I remembered those mornings —How great was that! I could even remember coming to the kitchen Christmas morning with my mother in the few years I had her, before she passed away.

After I gave Edna the piece of jewellery I had chosen for her and after she "oohd" and "aaahd", and put it on immediately, I opened my gift, a beautiful handmade throw in pinks and lilacs, knit of incredibly soft, silky yarn. A cup of tea, a few more dainties, a big hug and I was on my way. I wanted to hurry back quickly so the present opening could begin at Nate's. Nate and I were so looking forward to watching Mathilda's excitement when she opened her gifts. Nate would go pick Gran up later in the afternoon and she would stay to have supper with us.

I stopped at my condo on the way back to Nate's to pick up one of the presents for Mathilda I had forgotten. As I walked in the door the phone rang. I recognized the number, so I answered with a cheery "Merry Christmas Mr. Kelly." Which was met with complete silence, then a clearing of the throat, then Mr. Kelly saying, "Yes , it is a very Merry Christmas. I don't want to shock you but Jason is coming home. In a few days, after his health has been checked out and his credentials and identification verified, he will be on a flight home. Jason called me because he thought it might be a terrible shock for you to suddenly hear his voice. I was the contact for the ransom. So, the Saudis knew who I was. That is why they contacted me. Then Jason called.

I wanted to let you know right away. Jason asked that I tell you, so you can be with us when his plane lands. His story is a long story, and also a miracle. I will let him tell you himself when he is home. I know it's a shock. I'm hoping you still feel the same way about Jason and you will join us in welcoming him home. His plane lands this Friday at 3:00 p.m. We would be pleased if you would ride with us to the airport. Our limo will pick you up at 1:45 if that is agreeable?"

I could barely speak let alone think.

"Yes," I stammered. "I will be ready at 1:45. Thank you for including me. I don't know what to say. I have a million thoughts running through my mind. It really is a miracle. Thank you again for letting me know and including me."

Mr. Kelly's final comment was, "There is no way Jason would want to return home without seeing you waiting for him. "

After I hung up I thought, "What wonderful news. Jason is safe and coming home. And then I thought. I may have a big problem. If Jason is asking for me to be there, it's very unlikely he knows my life has moved on without him. How is this going to work out? I have to tell Nate. I have to tell him. But when? It will be quite a shock to give him the news that the previous love of my life has returned from the dead. And it seemed wrong to spoil the short time Nate was enjoying with a family he seldom sees. So, my decision will have to be to keep the news to myself until we are alone again, after his family has returned home."

My thoughts continued, "I owe it to Jason to meet him at the plane, and also to wait until he has started to recover from his ordeal before I tell him about Nate and I. Nate will see that I can't just hit Jason right away with the fact that I've moved on. Not after Jason has gone through a life-threatening kidnapping ordeal. And who knows what terrible conditions he suffered in order to survive? I will have to give Jason some time to settle in and find his feet, before I knock them out from under him. Nate is a very kind person and I know he will want me to do what's right."

I got through the Christmas festivities with Nate's family. And, I, along with everyone else, found joy in Mathilda's enchantment with everything Christmas. I got through all the great activities we had planned while Nate's family was with us. But the entire time Matilda, Sally, and Alex, were with us I felt like a fraud with a big black cloud of secrecy hanging over my head.

Nate's family went home on a late evening plane. When Nate and I were once again on our own, and Friday at 1:45 p.m. was looming, I sat with Nate and told him about Jason's return. I said I was planning to go to the plane with his family to greet him. Jason had asked for me to be there. He doesn't know about us. And I can't spring it on him the first day I see him. I'll have to give him some time before I tell him we're together.

Nate was silent for a minute (which seemed like an hour) before he said, " I'm shocked. It's amazing that he has returned. I can't even imagine what he must have gone through to survive a kidnapping in a place known for meting out wickedly severe punishments. In a country that has committed some terrible human rights atrocities.

Wherever Jason has been since the ransom was ignored, it's obvious he has had no opportunity to hear about how your life has changed."

I continued, "I'm sure Jason will be going somewhere for a short time to recover. I've decided if Jason has been doing well in recovery I will tell him about us on the first visit when I'm invited to see him. I can't lead him on thinking we will be together. That would be so wrong. He is someone, who at one time I truly loved. I am going to hate hurting him. I'm hoping telling him quickly will be best for him. Then he won't continue planning a life that includes me. He can make new decisions about how to go on with his life without me in it.

Nate spoke, "That seems like the right thing to do. For you too. It would be very difficult for you to be around Jason without him knowing about us. And it would definitely be unfair to Jason. He deserves to be told as soon as he has recovered enough to receive the news. I can certainly sympathize with how he's going to feel about losing you. I would never want to lose you. I need you here with me for life to be good. With those final words from Nate and a long, lingering kiss I said good-bye and drove back to my condo, to try to prepare for the next day's events. I was sure sleep would be elusive.

I spent the next morning getting ready for my 1:45 p.m. pick up by Jason's family. It was awful. I felt so dishonest. They were assuming things would be the same with Jason and me. I couldn't tell them things had changed. In my heart I knew before anyone else, I should tell Jason. Jason should be the first person I discussed with how my life had changed. And how Nate was the main part of that change. So, I "held my tongue", put aside my worry about how things would work out going forward, and tried to share the joy of Jason's return with his family. The air in the limo was so filled with the excitement and anticipation that radiated from every pore of his collective family it was almost smothering me. Finally, the ride that seemed never- ending came to an end. We all gathered at the arrival gate. And there coming across the tarmac from a private plane was Jason.

He was razor thin with long black hair, a short full black beard and a moustache. Though his walk was slow and measured I would have known him anywhere. A hand was on his elbow by his companion, who looked and walked very similarly to Jason.

Jason's family had put me at the forefront of the group. As Jason and his companion walked through the arrival gate Jason's eyes were only on me. He walked directly toward me. When he reached me he put his hands on my shoulders and for a few frozen seconds stood stock still just looking at me. Then he put his arms around me and pulled me close. The warm feeling of familiarity rushed back to me. As we stood together his arms tightened around me as if he would never let me go and he kissed me-a long, slow, curl your toes kind of kiss, that was so familiar it brought feelings of sweetness and remembered pleasure. Jason dropped his arm to my waist and we walked forward into the crush of his family together. He kept me by his side and with sudden feelings of guilt, I realized it felt good and right. That was very worrisome.

Jason turned to his travelling companion and introduced him as Ali, a true friend and life saver. Then Jason's dad took control. After all the hugs and greetings were over he herded everyone forward and organized everybody into the waiting family vehicles, as we no longer would all fit into a limo. Our little cavalcade headed to the Kelly's residence for a meal. After which Jason and Ali were going back to the city to settle into a private recovery clinic for several weeks to help them reintegrate back into normal society. There would be therapists and health care workers to help them reassess their life in Saudi Arabia and prepare them for their life back home. In Jason's case, it would be to fit back into the old life he had been living before Saudi Arabia. And in Ali's case it would be to fit into the new life he would be living after Saudi Arabia. Ali had been given asylum and the promise of eventual citizenship for his efforts to keep Jason alive and for the return of Jason safely home.

Before that next stage of their reintegration journey, after the meal, Jason and Ali wanted to tell their story while everyone was assembled together. So, as we did on that Christmas day which seemed so long ago, we filled the comfy sofas and chairs of the Kelly living room. On this day, although the location was the same, the shared joy of that Christmas day was now changed to a quieter joy because of Jason's return. After everyone was settled Jason began his story.

Jason said the day he arrived in Saudi Arabia, as he neared the exit door of the airport, two armed men hustled him out the door and into a waiting vehicle. He was blindfolded, and afraid for his life. He had no idea where he was going. Fear of the unknown is a powerful trigger for terror. And he definitely felt terror. After several hours when the blindfold was removed he saw that he was in a fenced enclave in the mountains. He saw many men who were either servicing weapons, doing menial chores, such as slicing vegetables in the outdoor kitchen, or just sitting in groups in the sun smoking and talking. All conversation stopped as Jason was marched in front of his two captors toward a man sitting in the shade who was obviously in charge. The man introduced himself as Mohammed Khan. He spoke very good English and addressed Jason saying, "Mr. Kelly, you may have guessed why you are here. We have no intention of harming you. We have arranged for a ransom to be paid within forty- eight hours for your release. Then you will be released back to the airport to continue on your way. While you are here you will be treated well. We may be outlaws but we are not animals. However, if you run my men will find you. When they bring you back you will be treated like an animal. Ali here will stay with you. Do as Ali says and you will be returned safely to your family. If you run you will never find your way out of these mountains. Throughout the years many men have found themselves lost and were never seen again. Ali will be your companion while you wait for the ransom drop. His

English is excellent. Please do not cause any problems. I would not wish to have you hurt. Do you understand?

I nodded my agreement, murmured yes, and was led away by Ali to get some food. We sat together in the shade to eat. He didn't speak and I didn't speak. I thought Ali seemed almost embarrassed to be part of this plan. Later I learned from Ali that this group was known as the Khan mafia. It was one of the largest outlaw organizations in Saudi Arabia. The mafia group was in trouble. Their finances were dwindling because a competing mafia group was taking over a lot of their business enterprises, businesses they had always controlled. So in the last few years kidnapping had been a way for this mafia group to keep their coffers full. As we sat in the shade that day Ali finally spoke telling me not to worry. Once the group received the ransom I would be free. That was somewhat reassuring

Nothing was that simple. The first night I was a captive the rival mafia group made a move on the Khan group. They breached the barricaded walls and started shooting and throwing Molotov cocktails. The Khan group I was with was caught unawares. They had to run moving higher into the mountains. Of course I had to run with them. For months the war between the Khan mafia and their enemies went on. The Khan mafia no longer had a permanent outpost. They were constantly on the move and I, with them. Everywhere we stopped to set up camp the rival mafia group caught up with us. And our group was dwindling as more and more of the fighters were killed. At first I was kept as a back-up plan so that whenever the fighting stopped or if the Khan group won, then the ransom deal could be on again. I could be bartered for cash. As time passed it seemed very unlikely the Khan mafia group would come out ahead in this war. And as everything was in turmoil I was basically forgotten, and Ali with me. Those in the Khan group, for all intensive purposes, were running for their lives. Ali and I were caught in the middle of a mafia war with two groups fighting for dominance in the Saudi mafia world.

Jason paused and looked over at Ali. He said" Ali would you prefer to tell your part of the story? Or should I continue on?

Ali nodded his approval for Jason to continue. So, Jason told how Ali had been recruited, not by choice, by the Khan mafia. The mafia had come to his village and had "Shanghaied" all the young men in the village forcing them to become part of the mafia group. Ali's older brother was not in the village. He had left to come to this country several years previously. Ali had all his paperwork ready to follow his brother. Ali had been approved to immigrate. When we escaped the Khan group, slipping away in the dead of night, at the height of the fighting and mass confusion, we worked our way out of the mountains by way of Ali's village. His mother had kept his immigration papers safe. She knew of the fighting and thought Ali was probably lost to her. She had kept the papers, living in hope, that someday he would return. With tears of joy and hugs from Ali's mother and sisters and with the precious papers tucked into Ali's least ripped jean pocket, we were on our way. After a torturous and clandestine journey over very rough terrain we made it to the closest Saudi embassy. Our first step to freedom.

Jason continued, "I owe my life, my very existence, to Ali. He will be staying with me at the recovery centre. Together we are going to work on getting past the terrible things he and I have seen and been part of. While with the mafia Ali was forced to keep the mafia vehicles serviced and in good running order. With all that experience he will fit in well at Kelly's Automotive and Towing. Ali is a very good mechanic. Although, no matter what he does he will always be like a brother to me."

Mr. Kelly spoke, "Ali you will always be a part of our family. We will forever love you like one of our own."

And with that everyone left their seats and came over to thank and hug Ali and to squeeze the life of out of Jason with tight hugs, gentle pats, cheek kisses, and quiet words. And I was enclosed in all of it as I stood within Jason's arm. It had been a long day for the two returnees, so Mr. Kelly, Mrs. Kelly, Ali, Jason, and I rode to the recovery centre. We waited until Ali and Jason were checked in. Then Mr. And Mrs. Kelly went out to the vehicle to wait for me. After they left Jason wrapped his arms around me pulling me close. And with soft words of love and hungry kisses he said good-bye to me. I promised after two weeks when the clinic thought it would be fine for me to visit, I would be there.

As I left to go to the Kelly's vehicle I felt I had to tell them the truth. There was no way I could keep up this pretence. They were very sad to hear my story, but very understanding too. I explained I wanted to wait to tell Jason until he was done with the first two weeks of the recovery program. I felt I would have to tell him immediately on my first visit. My life had changed and Jason deserved to know right away. It would be unfair, and unkind to Jason, to put off explaining why I couldn't be with him.

Mr. And Mrs. Kelly agreed. They said they would be sorry for Jason's loss and their loss too. They really were such kind people. In silence, each thinking our own thoughts, we drove to my condo. Mrs. Kelly hugged me as I was leaving the car and said she was sorry she would be losing a daughter. I was so touched the tears were going to start to fall so I just hugged her back and opened the door. The car waited until I entered the building. I took the elevator. Then I trudged into my condo to my lonely bedroom. I would be sleeping alone tonight. No warm love to keep me cozy. There was one love, Jason, I couldn't be with because time and distance had changed our lives. And there was one love, Nate, I couldn't be with, because of the other love, Jason, that with time and distance had changed our lives. Everything was a confused tangle.

As I lay waiting for sleep I knew it would be best to tell Jason about Nate on the first visit to see him at the clinic. I just couldn't pretend Jason and I were going to be together. Any little twitches of attraction that tried to entice me to feel the old feelings for Jason would just have to be ignored. I loved Nate and the sooner Jason knew that, the better it would be for all of us. And with that settled in my mind I turned off the light.

For the first two weeks Jason and Ali were to be totally immersed in programs at the recovery centre. It was suggested no phone calls should be made or received. At the end of two weeks Jason and Ali could invite visitors. What a godsend that was. No phone calls. I just couldn't imagine sharing loving phone calls for two weeks (essentially lying to Jason) until I could tell him about Nate. Both Jason and Ali seemed to have survived their ordeal surprisingly well, both mentally and physically. The conclusion was that their friendship and resilient personalities had helped them get through a time filled with danger and the constant fear of death. As they seemed to be doing well, I was hoping Jason would be mentally strong enough to take a blow about the end of our relationship.

I knew Mr. and Mrs. Kelly were going for their first visit to Jason and Ali in the morning of the third week. I would visit them in the afternoon. All morning I prepared myself for what I would say about Nate and how I would present the situation to Jason. I dressed in my best jeans and a sweater Edna had made me (for courage). I called a taxi, and went to the recovery clinic. When I got there Jason and Ali were waiting for me. As we sat in the private sitting room adjacent to Jason's rooms the three of us chatted for a few minutes. Then Ali said his goodbyes and left Jason and I alone. Jason and I were sitting on a love seat, he with his arm around me. I had to get it over with so before he could say anything I jumped in.

I said, "Jason I have something to tell you."

Jason interrupted quietly, "I know. I know something isn't right. I could tell from the first moment I held you. I was hoping I was mistaken. That maybe you just needed time to get used to us again. My worst fear was that you assumed I was gone forever and had found someone else. I hated that thought. I love you. My love for you kept me strong through everything in Saudi Arabia. My love for you never dimmed. No matter what the situation I knew I would get home to you. You were what I held onto for all those months. With me disappearing I can understand how it could happen. That you could find someone new and move on with your life. Logically I knew it could happen. I just didn't want to believe it was possible that I could ever lose you.

With tears in my eyes I tried to explain, "You were the love of my life. With no word about you and not knowing what had happened to you, I eventually had to accept that you were never coming back. The man I met just by chance is Nate. I met him one day when I returned to the crash scene. Nate was the anonymous person who found me and took me to the hospital. And as my crash did prove to be an attempted kidnapping he also helped capture the kidnappers, which in turn helped me to get my memory back. Nate and I have shared so much and he is a great guy. And I'm in love with him.

Jason looked into my eyes saying, "You deserve to be happy. I was just hoping against hope that I was imagining things. I knew something wasn't right, but I didn't want to believe it."

Jason went on, "You know I will always love you. I also know life changes. I'll wish you the best of everything and hope your life will be everything you've ever wanted. From being near death so many times these past months I know you should grab the good things in life and hold on. I never want to meet Nate. And I hope I never see you together. I don't think I could take that. But you have my love and I wish you only happiness."

And with that Jason turned me toward him, hugged me tight, and kissed me. Not our usual long, lingering kiss, but a short sweet goodbye kiss. Then he got up and walked away.

And somewhere along the way as I was walking toward the door I realized I missed that long, lingering kiss that was so familiar. That wasn't right. I shouldn't be missing Jason's kisses. I should be looking forward to Nate's. I squared my shoulders, went back to the condo, and called Nate. I said I would come right out to the resort to see him. I grabbed my bag, hopped in the car, and went to see my true love.

Nate was a man of many endearing qualities. Really, a great person to be with. He and I continued our relationship and enjoyed our life together. We went back to the routine of me staying with him on weekends at the resort, and me staying with him at his condo in the city when he could get away. The resort was thriving and as I did freelance work, I could work from anywhere. I sold my condo and moved to the resort permanently. Our planning was that Nate and I would have a small intimate marriage celebration there. I floated along on the tide of my relationship with Nate toward our eventual marriage. But when the time came to choose a wedding date it didn't seem right. And when I finally made myself sit down and seriously analyze my life I found that though I loved Nate and you couldn't find a better person to be with, something was holding me back from committing to marriage. And as I was sorting through my innermost feelings, I finally had to admit I still had some lingering feelings for Jason.

I decided I should see Jason again just to see how strong those lingering feelings were. I had tried to put Jason and our life together filed away in a folder of memories of the past. But at the most unexpected times my mind slipped back to those memories. At first I tried to tell myself it was natural to have memories resurface from time to time of someone who had been so important to me. But, I was with Nate and I loved him. And it seemed very disloyal to be thinking of Jason as much as I had been. Could it be the permanence of my upcoming marriage to Nate that was causing me to critically reassess my future? Whatever was causing my sudden indecision, I was sure removing Jason from my thoughts was at least part of the solution. I made a plan. The first thing I would do was drive by Kelly's Automotive and Towing. Then if I could get up the courage I would go in and see Jason, and either erase, or admit, that I still had feelings for him.

On a fine sunny day I drove to Kelly's Automotive and Towing. As I sat looking at Jason's place it did bring a tiny twinge of longing for what had been. I made up my mind. I would go in to say "hello" and decide then and there whether I had any feelings of deep love left for Jason. (It felt very wrong to be doing this when Nate trusted my love implicitly). I had convinced myself that in a way I was doing this for Nate too. Just as I started to get out of the car I saw Jason and a tall, striking, blonde come walking out the door. She was not only striking. Her jacket, dress, shoes, and bag, were the trappings of wealth. Jason was walking the woman to a car parked at the curb. Before the woman got into her car she and Jason embraced and shared a pretty hot looking kiss.

I didn't like it. Which was so wrong. I had left Jason for Nate. And I couldn't have found a better person than Nate. And I loved Nate. How could I possibly have such a strong reaction to Jason kissing someone else? That kiss was the catalyst. My heart sank. Realization hit me like a sledgehammer. I had given up something I shouldn't have. I had given up Jason out of a sense of loyalty and what I thought was true and total love for Nate.

Let there be no mistake. I had loved Nate truly and with my whole being. At least I believed I had. I thought my love for Nate was solid and unshakeable. The revelation about me still having feelings for Jason was not good. It seemed impossible. I thought those feelings were safely put away in the past. The reoccurrence of feelings for Jason was going to ruin the path of complete happiness I had set for myself with Nate. Nate's deep love for me was what few people would ever experience. And I couldn't believe I was seriously considering giving that up.

I went back to Nate's condo which we now shared when in the city. I sat on a hard kitchen chair and took a hard look at my life. Was it possible I had fallen so completely for Nate because of our strong connection through a series of very traumatic events? There were so many connections to my accident between Nate and I. He had not only saved my life by taking me to the hospital at great risk to himself. He had also removed the threat of my kidnapping by organizing a plan to apprehend the kidnappers. And more than that, Nate had also been present for one of the most momentous moments of my life. He was there when my world enlarged, as I found my memory, and my past returned. Were all these events that had brought Nate and I together the basis for our love? And was that a good enough basis for a life together? I knew Nate was much more than these connections. I could not diminish what we had by thinking our caring for each other only grew because of a series of events threaded together. Yet, still my mind kept going in circles. Maybe I had been fooling myself about the strength of my love for Nate. And maybe that was the reason I couldn't commit to a wedding date.

Seeing Jason again and seeing him with someone else had changed things. And why should it change things? Why should it bring back feelings for him if I was secure in my feelings for Nate? I told myself to "get over it". I tried to tell myself I was overreacting to Jason's lingering kiss with the expensive- looking blonde. I loved Nate. I was happy with Nate. We had a life planned together. Nate never was a second choice. He had been a lovely alternative to Jason after Jason was gone. I didn't like these feelings of doubt and confusion. I didn't like that there was confusion in my mind. I had to be absolutely sure of any decision I might make, before taking any action I might forever regret.

As I had grown to love Nate, I had grown to love his outdoor world. I had enjoyed all the outdoor activities our life included. I had enjoyed those activities on their own merit but mostly I enjoyed them, because I shared those activities with Nate. If I wasn't with Nate I would not only miss him, but I'd miss the life we had built together. I would miss the late night bonfires, in a forest where the night animals quietly go about their nightly routines, where the huge pines are like a green wall of protection, and where these amazing things are all bundled under a canopy of starlight, their sparkle unhindered by the lights of civilization. If I went to Jason the pain I would cause Nate would lie heavy on my heart.

After the agony and anguish of coming to a decision I finally admitted to myself my continuing feelings for Jason. I knew I had to end it with Nate. I knew it would be awful. How could I possibly disappoint and deeply hurt a man who had made my world so very nearly perfect.

The morning after the lightning revelation of my feelings for Jason I travelled out to the resort to see Nate. We sat together at the huge oak table in the sunny open kitchen and I told him. I told him how sorry I was. And how much he meant to me. How I never could have believed this would ever happen. As I finished speaking Nate didn't say anything immediately.

After a long silent pause he said, "I felt a connection to you from the moment I laid you carefully in the box of my truck, after coming upon the crash site. That surprising feeling of connection was there as I cared for you all day, before I took you to the hospital that night. And I couldn't believe my good fortune the afternoon I came upon you stopped at the edge of the road, at the scene of your crash. It was like it was meant to be. I had looked for you but you had disappeared. I could not find Serafina Douglas. Suddenly seeing you on the road, in the exact spot where I had found you that day, was like a dream being realized.

He continued, "I guess as a grown-up I should have realized that dreams seldom come true. I can't believe it. I found you and now I've lost you. When Jason returned I was afraid that might be the end of us. I watched for signs that possibly you weren't completely over him. You seemed exactly the same, so I put my fears to rest and just enjoyed our life. I had proclaimed myself the winner of your love. It seems I was over-confident. I love you so much and I know you love me. I don't know how you can go. I don't believe this is happening. I know you love me, but apparently not enough."

Then Nate continued, "It seems there is nothing I can say. If that's the way it will be I will have to accept it. Just know that I'll be right here if you ever want to find your way back to us."

As I stumbled to leave the kitchen I said, " I'm sorry. I'm so sorry. I didn't know I would ever hurt you. I thought we would be together forever." As I turned to leave I could barely see through eyes filled with tears. And with a tear- thickened voice I said I would come back during the week to pick up my things. As I stepped out into the sunshine my words fell upon heavy, deafening, silence.

In some ways it was very foolish to end my future life with Nate when I had no idea if Jason was serious about the expensive blonde, or in fact, anyone else. But staying with Nate and loving him less than Jason would be so wrong. Nate had been much more than a replacement for Jason. He had been a wonderful gift to my life while Jason was gone. But Jason had returned.

Fortunately I had a place to stay now I would no longer be staying with Nate. My friend Julie was away in Europe. She had kindly offered me the use of her place after I told her I was going to leave Nate. With great surprise and sadness at my announcement, Julie said, "Are you sure? Are you sure you can give up your life with Nate? You two always seemed to be so good together. "

I said, "We were. But Jason came back and no matter how wonderful Nate is he is not Jason." After that comment we then ended our conversation with her offer of her apartment and a sign off of " good luck hon.'"

When I got to Julie's I just sat in place. I felt numb. What a "hash" I had made of my life. I'd gambled on Jason still wanting me without the slightest inkling of proof that might be true. Now at two different times I'd left hurt and sadness in the lives of the two people who had meant the most to me. And now I was going to try and reverse that hurt and sadness for one of them. If he still wants me.

To end one life and revive another I must first go to Nate's resort to get my things. Neither Nate nor I would be able to move on with reminders of me in the home which would now be his alone. The more quickly I removed my things, the less painful it would be for both of us.

I returned to the resort two days after my bombshell "dumping" of Nate. There was no getting around it, that's what I had done, although in the softest way I could. I had dealt Nate a heart-wrenching blow. I was doing what my heart told me to do. However, the sadness I felt at hurting this man I had grown to love was unbelievably deep.

I had chosen a day to collect my things when I knew Nate wouldn't be home. I'm sure he as much as I, didn't want to be together for the closing of our final chapter. Nate always met his lifelong friend George, the local bank manager, for coffee every Wednesday morning.

Consequently, when Wednesday morning came I was driving down the "oh, so familiar road", into the forest to Nate's lovely resort.

Chapter Thirteen:
The surprise of my life!

As I saw the familiar buildings, the beautiful landscaping, and the perfect serenity of this still, quiet place, the only sound I heard was the twitter of sparrows in the trees as they heralded my arrival. My stomach lurched. Had I done the right thing? Could I really give up all this, this life, and Nate? I had been living a dream in every way that counted.

I was giving up a kind, attentive, handsome, man who loved me. I was giving up a life that was calm, satisfying, and filled with the enjoyment an outdoor lifestyle can bring. And as I walked to the front entrance of the resort my sense of purpose wavered for just a moment. Then I patted the big old house cat sitting in the rocker by the top step. I put my key in the brass key lock of the handsome deep blue door. I pushed the door open and entered the spacious, cheery, kitchen to the left of the entrance.

What a scene of destruction! The kitchen looked like it had been torn apart! Obviously something had gone very wrong in this house. My senses were screaming to back up and get out!

But what if Nate was there? What if he was hurt or injured? On the other hand, what if someone was still in the house? If that was the case what could I do to help Nate on my own? I backed out through the open doorway and crept around the side of the building to the pool house. I knew there was a phone there. I called the police, explained the situation, then stayed perfectly still, hidden in a corner of the pool house which was not touched by sunlight from either the glass door or the large windows.

After what seemed like an eternity but surprisingly, by my watch, was mere minutes, I heard cars pulling up onto the wide, pebble-covered, driveway, then doors quietly closing. Immediately a police officer was gently tapping on the pool house door. I hurried out of my secure corner to hear what he had to say. Before he could speak I stuttered out, "It's terrible in the house. The kitchen is torn apart. It was frightening to see. I'm so glad you got here quickly."

The police officer explained that he and his officers arrived so quickly because they were already on their way to the resort when my call was received. Earlier, several of Nate's closest neighbours had reported hearing rapid fire gunshots coming from the forested area at the outer edge of the resort.

He continued, "We don't take reports of gunshots lightly. They are a "priority first" call. Unfortunately, on our way to investigate the gunshots our progress came to a standstill caused by a three car pile up on a bad curve on the highway. Luckily all injuries from the crash were minor. However, it caused quite a delay for us. We had to back down the highway until we could access an alternate road to reach the resort, which took us considerably longer than planned. But, that made or arrival almost coincide with your call.

The officer then said he and his three men were going to check out the house and surrounding area. I was to wait where I was until he returned to give me the "all clear".

As I waited the still, hard, silence continued. I heard no sounds of life or movement as the officers stealthily did their job. Suddenly, the silence was broken by a series of gunshots. These gunshots seemed to be much closer to the house than the first gunshots reported by the neighbours as having come from the outer edge of the property.

Although never having been around guns I definitely recognized the sound of gunshots. The sound was familiar because I had heard the sound several times recently, when Nate's groundskeeper had taken a few shots at a coyote. The coyote had been skulking around the property looking for lunch, killing small animals like squirrels, gophers, and mice. That same coyote had been skulking around the big, old, overly plump, house cat where he was as usual, holding court from the large wooden rocker on the patio that graced the front entrance. These shots however were different than those of the groundskeeper. They were shot in rapid succession. These sounded very close to the house and therefore very close to the pool house! They were scary!!

At the first sound of the gunshots I had crouched down, and crab-walked as quickly as a person can crab- walk, back into my secure corner hidden from sight. I crouched not moving a muscle waiting for either more shots, or for the officer to come back to the pool house. It seemed like an interminable amount of time, but finally the officer returned. He said the house was empty. He said the shots came from the forested area on the property that was closest to the house. So, I should stay in the pool house. Two of his officers were going to check out the area around the house.

The officer continued, saying there were several probable reasons Nate could be away from the property. "He could be away dealing with everyday affairs as usual. That could be ascertained by a few phone calls."

He then added, "We also have to consider the fact that Nate may actually be missing, or involved in the shootings. But really it is too soon to panic." The thought that Nate might be involved in the shootings was frightening and extremely worrying.

The senior police officer requested that I phone Nate's friends and acquaintances and hopefully find out where Nate was. He then assigned a very young police officer to stay with me. The police officer looked to be about fifteen. He certainly didn't instill confidence. Though I knew he would have to be qualified to be on the force. As the very young officer stood guard at the door I used the pool house phone, hurriedly squatting on the floor out of sight, after dialling. I called everyone I could think of who might be with Nate. The answers were all the same. "No, they hadn't seen him".

A thorough search had proven definitely that no one was now in the house. Also the forested area was proven to be clear of any shooters. The officers had found no sign of anyone. But they did see a dark grey SUV take off across a pasture in the distance.

Because it could be a robbery attempt gone wrong, the senior police officer asked if I would come into the house and take a look around to see if anything was missing. Although, if it was a robbery, what about the gunshots after the supposed robbers had left the house? The only probable reason for those shots, and it was very alarming, was that the shots had something to do with Nate being missing.

I tucked my fears away temporarily, forced myself to walk through the front door, then step into the kitchen. The senior police officer cautioned me not to touch anything and then handed me a pair of disposable booties to cover my shoes. That was unsettling. In the movies and on TV that's what the police did when investigating a serious crime scene—like murder. That thought scared me to death. It was a terrifying thought.

As I entered the kitchen details I hadn't noticed when previously entering, then exiting so suddenly, shocked me. I was aghast at what I saw. Shining, glossy, and brightly lit by the light from the kitchen window was a small puddle of blood. It was pooled by the corner of the counter and there were also bloody marks going toward the side door. It looked like something had been pulled or dragged across the floor. My blood chilled, my mind froze, my heart started pounding like a jackhammer. Where was Nate? And whose blood was that? It was in Nate's kitchen so that could mean something very bad.

The senior police officer could see my terror and tried to calm me by saying the blood was not necessarily Nate's. There could be other explanations. His vague assertion wasn't helping me. I couldn't go any further into the house. I removed the booties and went to sit absolutely motionless on a bench at the edge of the patio. The young officer who had been assigned to me stayed near me for several minutes. He then wandered slightly away from me, looking toward where the recent gunshots had originated, then wandered farther away to talk to another officer.

And that's when I heard it. "Annie". Did I really hear something? Then I heard it again, "psst, Annie". I started to look around trying to see anything that would help me locate where the whisper was coming from. I looked toward the bushes near the patio. I looked toward the side of the house. I looked toward the driveway behind the parked vehicles. And finally my eyes settled on the tall thick mass of decorative grasses planted to hide the building's cement foundation. That ghostly little whisper came once again, "Annie", preceded by "psst". That's where the sound was coming from-from those tall grasses. It had to be Nate. If it wasn't that would be extremely creepy and very frightening. Who else could it be? Who would be whispering my name except Nate? Not likely to be a bad guy or the shooter.

The pounding of my heart slowed, my spirits rose. The hands I had been holding tightly clenched together unclenched. I took a closer look at the thick grasses around the foundation.

Sure enough, if I really looked and concentrated I could see a very fine sliver of blue in amongst the grasses. Likely from a familiar denim shirt. The whisperer continued, "Meet me at the big old oak tree by the waterfall tonight at dusk. I'm sure you'll remember."

I looked around to see if anyone was watching me. Then I whispered back, "Nate, are you hurt? Should you be getting medical help? There's blood on the kitchen floor."

Nate replied, in a barely discernible whisper, "No, I'm fine. This morning before I left for town I made a pot of coffee thinking I'd have a cup with my breakfast. Then I went upstairs to dress. When I came back downstairs two overgrown muscle men were waiting in my kitchen. They were very familiar. They were part of the crime ring I had been hiding out from, when I found you injured at the side of the road all those months ago."

Nate continued," I have to get out of here. Just please meet me tonight and I'll explain everything."

I whispered "yes" to the silent grasses and saw the sliver of blue disappear from view. The first step in helping Nate was to leave the property. So, I motioned to the young officer. When he came to where I was sitting I asked if he would check with the senior officer to see when I could leave. The senior officer came across the patio to stand beside me. He said I was free to go, but I must come to the station house the next day to give a formal statement. I thanked him, made my way to my car, turned it around, passed the empty police cars, and left the resort.

The first order of business was to rent an inconspicuous beige sedan to use to pick up Nate. My bright blue SUV was too noticeable and recognizable. That done, I went to my friend Julie's apartment to wait until dusk would be descending upon the forest. Julie's apartment would be a secure place for Nate to stay until the DEA stepped in. My plan was to drop Nate at the apartment. Then I would leave to stay in a hotel for the few days Nate might be at Julie's. I just couldn't live with Nate again. Not after what I had done. If I stayed at the apartment Nate and I would be sharing a very tense, sad, space. Really, any length of time to be together now would be too long, if you factored in my guilt and Nate's hurt. And although he never said a word about it, I'm sure Nate felt anger at what could be considered the unfairness of what I had done.

I was sure the DEA would act quickly. Though, if they didn't act quickly I would be Nate's connection to the outside world. Then my "clean break" leading to a new life with Jason would be put on hold. And way in the back recesses of my mind was a guilt-ridden thought. If Nate's necessary stay at the apartment dragged on, I might lose my window of opportunity for getting Jason back. It seemed so selfish to be thinking like that when Nate was in danger. I would just have to hope the DEA would come through quickly. And of course Nate's safety was not to be forgotten. His very life was in danger. So, I put thoughts of meeting Jason away temporarily until Nate was safe.

As the late afternoon started to lose its bright sunlight and dusk started to settle in, I drove out to the farthest edge of Nate's property. The property line was several miles from the resort proper. I travelled down a narrow pasture path to the big old oak tree to meet Nate. Nate had said "I'm sure you'll remember," leaving the words hanging.

I sure did remember. I knew his location because at the end of that dirt road was a little waterfall that fell into a pool full of fat little trout. Nate and I had often spent the afternoon on the edge of the pool catching trout for supper. And because the spot was "end of the earth" secluded we often had a blanket with us. And as you may have guessed, this totally secluded spot on Nate's property, the dappled sunshine peeking through the leaves of the big old oak tree, and the soft background of water falling from the little waterfall, led to wonderful romance of unforgettably epic proportions.

Then as the day waned we gathered our clothes and once more became presentable for polite society. We retrieved our string of fish and went home for a late afternoon fish fry, giving our extra catch to the two young gardeners Nate employed.

I'm sure they enjoyed the fish, but not nearly as much as we enjoyed the afternoon catching them!

As I continued along the skinny little pasture road with wild, untamed, tangled, bushes on each side, my mind wandered back to those monumentally wonderful times with Nate.

In my mind I was totally and absolutely sure about Jason being the man I wanted to be with. Though, when you think someone might be dead, it can make you re-assess a decision you made while that person was alive, look at that decision through a different lens, with a different perspective. Did I make the right decision? Yes, I did.

Going to the old oak tree, waterfall, and pool, to a place with such great past memories I'll admit might have brought a tiny niggling bit of doubt about leaving Nate. It was so very tiny I quickly removed it from my mind, replaced it with Jason's smile, and drove on to my clandestine meeting with Nate.

And there he was standing, watching for me. He was barely discernible, by the huge oak tree on the shore of the tiny pool. There was some moonlight partially covered by cloud but still giving enough light to make out Nate's form. As I left the car and walked toward him it was like deja vu of times past. When I got close enough to see him looking at me, the look he was giving me was a look I had seen many times. It showed pure love and it made the choice I had made to leave him seem unthinkably cold. Then as quickly as I had seen the look, it was gone, and Nate was all business saying, " I'll explain what happened today."

So in that deep, smooth voice I had always found so appealing, he explained. "My DEA days caught up with me. As I told you I went downstairs to have my morning coffee. And there casually sprawled in my kitchen chairs were two extremely ugly gorillas. They were cousins. As I mentioned, they were part of the criminal group I had been hiding out from, at the time I found you by the side of the road. I went over to the counter and poured myself some coffee, then remained standing by the coffee pot.

To save themselves from prosecution and evade long jail terms these two thugs had turned on their buddies, associates, and their family, to "save their own skins". They had testified against the men in the criminal organization they had been a part of. Because their testimony assured prosecution of their criminal associates, the two men were then offered immunity and a placement in the WIT SEC program, also called the Witness Security Program. As the two thugs relaxed casually around my kitchen table they proceeded to tell me they were very unhappy in the WIT SEC program. They hated their low status, and dead end jobs. They hated the cities they had been placed in. They didn't like to be away from their families and friends. Mostly, they missed having large amounts of cash from the profits of crime, to fund the luxurious lifestyles they had previously been accustomed too.

And although they were supposed to have absolutely no contact with anyone from their old life, somehow they had managed to contact each other. As both were totally disgruntled with the life they had been given they planned to go back to their old ways. Although realistically, that old life would likely be very short. Criminal gangs have a long reach and a long memory. To my way of thinking the two will be dead within a week. They were unimportant, and negligible, the rag-tag end of the group and the least smart or valuable members. They now are a problem that will be easily solved. I'm sure death is in their immediate future.

These two thugs had somehow forgotten that they had escaped an endless prison term to have a "normal life" by "ratting" out their associates. But apparently fear of death from former cohorts was less awful than a "normal" life. Apparently nothing could be worse than being stuck in a "normal life" forever. In their minds I was the cause of all their problems because I had talked them into taking the WIT SEC deal. They wanted retribution. And I was it. In their minds removing me was their start to a new beginning.

When the thugs were done whining they decided to make their move. One thug grabbed my arm and his cousin joined him. In the scuffle that ensued everything in the kitchen went flying. I managed to grab the coffee pot full of boiling, hot, coffee. I threw all the boiling coffee from the pot onto the first thug. Then I hit the one closest to me, near the counter, in the head with the heavy metal pot. He went down in a cloud of blood. Then, as one was trying to see through the boiling coffee dripping down his face, and the other lay bleeding on the floor I took off through the side door ".

I said, "But Nate, we heard several gunshots."

"Yes", Nate explained, "when I first made it into the forest one thug had followed me. He had seen which direction I'd gone and let off a few pot shots in that direction to try to force me out of my hiding spot. Thankfully he only hit tree trunks and sent tree bark flying. Those were the first shots fired.

I'm assuming the thug realized someone may have heard those shots, so he turned and hustled back to the house. I followed at a safe distance and saw him return to the kitchen, drag his buddy out of the house, and with great difficulty stuff his buddy into the back seat of a dark grey SUV parked near the side door. They then took off at full speed toward the resort exit. I kept watching them. When they reached the resort exit road they stopped. They parked where they had a clear view of the house, out of sight in some trees and large bushes. From where they were parked they could obviously see you arrive and then see the entire police force arrive in their three cop cars. These thugs should have been on their way. But they were reckless and vengeful and wanted one last chance to get rid of me. They waited patiently out of sight and their wait paid off.

The thugs caught sight of me heading to the house. They let off a series of shots hoping they could make the hit on me. They knew the peril of their position. There were police officers already on the property, but they really wanted me dead. After that last failed attempt they wheeled around and headed across an open pasture in the direction of the main road."

"Yes," I added, "When I arrived I went into the house and saw the wreckage. I hurriedly backed out of the house and called the police from the pool house. The dispatcher said the police were on their way. Someone had called to report repeated rapid gunshots in the area.

Nate continued , "Yes, those were the shots from the first time they had tried to kill me. I felt I could make it closer to the house without being seen. I wanted to check on the police activity and assess the situation. I was not as invisible as I tried to be. The thugs caught sight of me and let off another volley of shots on the off chance they could make the hit. When that didn't work and they had given away their position they hurriedly took off at great speed across the pasture. The one police car dispatched to chase them would never have caught them. It would be like a donkey chasing a panther, with no hope of success.

When I saw you walk away from the house to sit on the bench I made my way around the back of the house and slipped into the tall grasses covering the foundation. I didn't want to be seen by the local cops. I'm staying out of sight until I can contact the DEA. I will have to disappear until these two thugs are apprehended by law enforcement, and this time sent to jail. Or until the two are killed by any other criminal organization that does not want the focus of the law turned onto them, by the unhinged antics of two wild cards. The DEA is much better equipped to handle two return members of a now disabled infamous crime organization, who will now be looking to join a new group. The three car police detachment in this area couldn't handle a case this serious. They don't have the expertise or manpower. Shots fired and blood mysteriously smeared on a kitchen floor are events these local cops, have seldom, if ever been called upon to deal with.

So, if you can help me get to a place to stay until I can sort things out and contact the DEA you literally, possibly, may be a life saver. I nodded and started to the car with Nate following behind. This returned togetherness was uncomfortable already, yet so familiar. I hated to think how uncomfortable things would be if we had to spend too much time together. As we reached the car I turned and said. "You know I'd do anything to help you if you were in trouble."

Nate quietly replied, "Thank you. I do," as he silently slipped onto the floor of the backseat of the car.

As we drove I explained Julie had offered me the use of her apartment while she was away when she heard of our break-up. It was hard to say those words. And the comment from the backseat of "I wouldn't classify it as our break-up" made me saying the words seem harsh and cold.

After a ride "full to overflowing with silence" we finally arrived at Julie's place. During the day after I had picked up the rental car, I had gone out to get Nate a change of clothes, some necessities, and a large back pack. I'd also stocked the fridge. I bought some beer for Nate figuring he might need some kind of a drink after the day he had been through. As we reached the doorway of the apartment I explained that I was staying at a hotel for the night.

I said," I thought that would be the best arrangement for both of us."

Nate nodded and replied, "Thanks for coming to get me. You really may be a lifesaver. I hope I won't have to keep you out of your friend's apartment for too long. I am immediately going to contact the DEA. Tomorrow by noon I should be gone."

I once again said, " You know I'd do anything for you."

Then I turned and quickly scurried down the hall and out of sight. I knew we both did not want to share another long good-bye.

In my hotel room I watched all the newscasts. Without much detail, the announcers told of shots being fired at Nate's resort and that the owners were not at home at the time of the incident. I was assuming as the DEA would be taking over the case they had instructed the local police not to release many details.

The evening dragged on. When I finally turned off the TV and tried to sleep, my thoughts focused on Nate and Jason. I felt like a criminal, full of guilt about the break up I'd caused.

Although to be fair about the choice I'd made, the break-up never would have happened if there hadn't been the miracle of Jason's return. In that part of the equation I was blameless. But still the feeling of guilt remained. I felt sadness and regret that although Nate had loved me totally, it wasn't enough. I hadn't loved him enough. And therefore there would be a lot of hurt for him, knowing he was being replaced.

What made it worse was that I would do anything to help Nate. He deserved nothing less, but I had this little underlying fear that kept re-surfacing. What if Nate needed my help as his connection to the outside world for too long? What if the DEA for some reason didn't want to extract him from the apartment to another safe house right away? And what if in the meantime Jason met someone else. I didn't know how I would make my future life work if that were to happen. If I lost my chance to re-unite with Jason I would live my life drowning in a sea of regret.

It never came to that. When I arrived at the apartment the next morning there was coffee ready on the counter. Nate was up and had obviously already showered because his hair was slicked back wet and he looked so handsome, as he always did. Those looks were something I could always appreciate but which would not influence my choice of another. Nate was sitting on the bench by the door finishing putting on his boots just as there was a knock at the door. When he opened the door their stood Devon and Matt his old DEA partners and friends. They greeted me with "nice to see you Annie". They didn't come in.

As they stood at the doorway Nate grabbed his new backpack and turned to me. He walked across the floor to me. Put his arms around me and held me in a gentle embrace while he said softly, "Thank you for everything. Thank you for helping me. Thank you for the life we've shared. And remember. Eventually I'll be back at the resort. If you change your mind you'll know where to find me. He kissed my lips good-bye, then stepping through the doorway and softly closing the door behind him, he was gone.

Sadness overwhelmed me. Again tears came; for the closing of a chapter, for the ending of something that had enhanced my life in so many ways.

Then I wiped my tears away and with fresh purpose and determined resolve I decided how to re-build my life with Jason. No matter how much I had loved Nate, somewhere hidden deep, lurking quietly, had been my love for Jason. And now I was going to do something about it.

The next day I packed away my sadness and tears about the break-up with Nate. And although some of those feelings lingered very slightly, my heart and mind was laser focused on the anticipation, hope, and absolute ecstasy of seeing Jason again. I know it seemed wrong to rush to Jason the minute Nate was gone. I couldn't wait. Jason and I could not make up for lost time. But we could start again.

So, at 9:30 a.m. the morning after Nate left, on a day that was bright with sunshine and when the leaves were turning, I walked through the front door of Kelly's Automotive and Towing, and then into the sunroom out back. There was Jason standing by the coffee maker. When he looked up I could see the surprise in his eyes. Then I could see the welcome and love. He came toward me and put his arms around me.

He said, "It was you. It was always you. And it always will be you." And with that he kissed me and I was home.

Oh, I did find out about the blonde who had been trying to convince Jason she was the one. And I did tell him about my terrible feelings of regret about hurting Nate. But I also made it very clear with words and actions that I knew I had made the right choice.

For me: it was Jason. My heart had always kept a place for Jason tucked away in a corner, never giving up that spot saved for him, even when things had looked bleak for his return. Though Nate was a wonderful man in so many ways, I couldn't remove Jason from that special place in my heart.

I do not see Nate. I'm sure it's by his choice as much as mine. He no longer belongs to the card club and I have never run into him in the city. With deep and true feeling I wish him the best in life, and hope he finds a love he deserves. As I did.

Chapter Fourteen:
A Good Ending

Jason and I have found our way. Often if Jason arrives home before me I am greeted by the delicious aroma of something cooking. My handsome husband with his jet black hair, cut short and crisp, his clear blue eyes and his tall, athletic form is waiting for me. Still dressed in his classy executive work clothes; tonight his blue dress shirt has the sleeves rolled up to the elbows and the classic black dress pants he is still wearing speak of quiet wealth. He looks what he is, a very successful businessman.

However, if you look closely you will see this top-notch executive is comfortably at home. You will notice he is standing by the stereo in his black dress socks where he's intently picking the perfect record to welcome me home. He places the needle on the vinyl. The soft melody starts to play. Jason turns to me. He opens his arms. I glide into them. And we dance.

Sometimes your first true love, through adversity and change, remains your best true love.

ABOUT THE AUTHOR

The author's name is Sandra. She has always been called Cindy, never Sandra, which has caused much confusion throughout her life.

Her career was as a teacher, teaching grades (K-8). After she retired, she taught Sociology, on a contractual basis, at a secondary education school for six years.

Cindy is a painter selling her art locally under the name S. I. Wilson.

Cindy has had several romance/mystery novels published. Their titles are: "Butterscotch Mints, Murder and Romance", "Every Seven Years", and "I Don't Remember".

She has also has written a children's book, "Three Bunny Brothers and a Big Yellow Dog" now published. It is "Book 1" in a series of 4 "Bunny Brothers" books.

Cindy has always been a reader. She has always loved libraries.

ABOUT THE BOOK

TWO BOOKS:
"Every Seven Years"
and
"I Don't Remember"

Each book is a love story:
Each book has true love:

Each story takes place in the 1960's:

In "Every Seven Years"

One summer a young American draft dodger named Mitch, finds a special love named Katie, at a Canadian lake. They know their love will last forever. Then suddenly, and without warning, their path to forever is thrown into disrepair by circumstances they cannot control.

In "I Don't Remember"

A wealthy young woman named Annie is injured and her memory disappears. She starts her life over when a very special man named Jason steps into her life. Their love is " over the top " wonderful, strong, and true. Unfortunately, their perfect life does not remain perfect when life takes an unexpected turn.

There are many similarities in both books:

Each book has a disappearance:
Each book has a new love found, then lost:
Each book suddenly has a new love enter the picture:
Each book has a reunion:
In each book there is a difficult choice to be made:

In each book: "One true love wins out in the end"

(Suitable for ladies from twelve to one hundred and twelve)

Printed in the USA
CPSIA information can be obtained
at www.ICGtesting.com
CBHW031720241024
16327CB00023B/252